The Trials of Hairy-Clees

CRiSPiN BOYER

Illustrated by Andy Elkerton

UNDER THE *Stars*

NATIONAL GEOGRAPHIC

Published by National Geographic Partners, LLC.

NATIONAL GEOGRAPHIC and Yellow Border Design are trademarks of the National Geographic Society, used under license.

Under the Stars is a trademark of National Geographic Partners, LLC.

Since 1888, the National Geographic Society has funded more than 14,000 research, conservation, education, and storytelling projects around the world. National Geographic Partners distributes a portion of the funds it receives from your purchase to National Geographic Society to support programs including the conservation of animals and their habitats. To learn more, visit natgeo.com/info.

For more information, visit nationalgeographic.com, call 1-877-873-6846, or write to the following address:

National Geographic Partners, LLC
1145 17th Street N.W.
Washington, DC 20036-4688 U.S.A.

For librarians and teachers: nationalgeographic.com/books/librarians-and-educators

More for kids from National Geographic: natgeokids.com

National Geographic Kids magazine inspires children to explore their world with fun yet educational articles on animals, science, nature, and more. Using fresh storytelling and amazing photography, *Nat Geo Kids* shows kids ages 6 to 14 the fascinating truth about the world—and why they should care. **kids.nationalgeographic.com/subscribe**

For rights or permissions inquiries, please contact National Geographic Books Subsidiary Rights: bookrights@natgeo.com

Designed by Amanda Larsen
Hand-lettering by Jay Roeder

Hardcover ISBN: 978-1-4263-3896-0
Reinforced library binding ISBN: 978-1-4263-3897-7

Printed in the United States of America
21/WOR/1

To Betty the brave

—C.B.

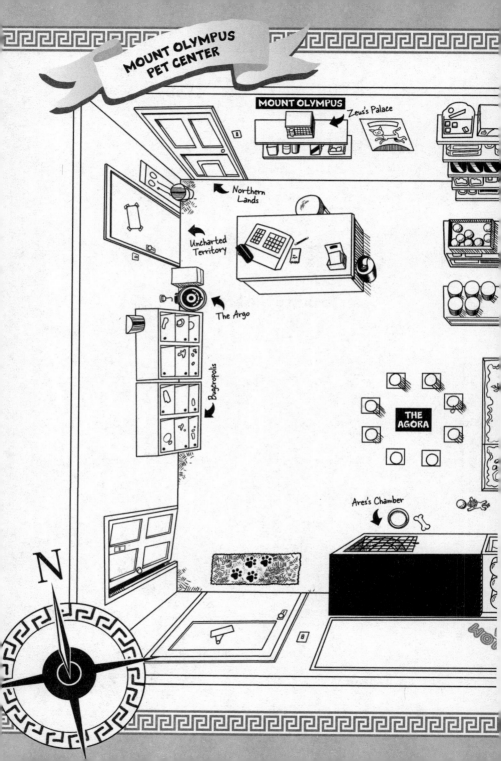

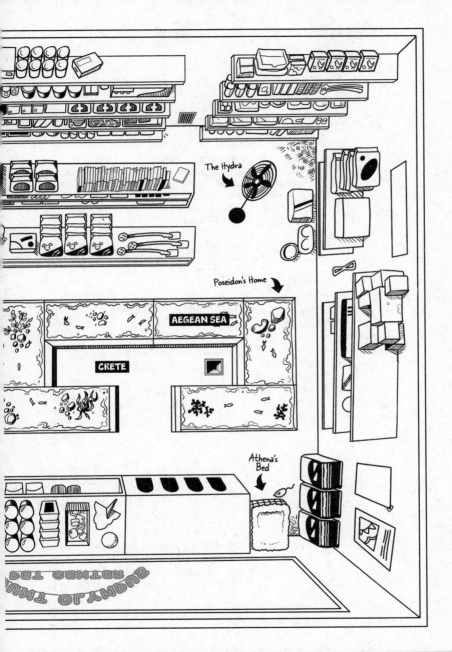

Zeus is a golden hamster with a cloud-shaped patch on his cheek. Zeus believes he's the king of all the other animals that live at the Mount Olympus Pet Center. The favorite rescued pet of Artie, the shop's owner, Zeus genuinely cares about his fellow Olympians but also sees them as minions that should follow him on nightly adventures, which often go awry. When humans aren't around, he scrambles down from "Mount Olympus," the highest shelf in the shop where his enclosure is, and pictures himself wearing a white chiton—a fine shirt people wore in ancient Greece—and a crown-like gilded laurel wreath.

Demeter is a small grasshopper with a big heart. Once a resident of the rescue center's Bugcropolis (the city of insects), she's now Zeus's constant, loyal companion and loves to explore the shop's world. She wears a sash of lettuce over her shoulder and a laurel wreath on her head to represent the Greek goddess of the harvest, for whom she's named. The youngest and fastest of the Olympians, Demeter can fly in short bursts. But don't let her size fool you—this is one courageous grasshopper!

Athena is the wise gray tabby cat that lives under the front window of Mount Olympus Pet Center. Named after the goddess of wisdom, Athena often tries to keep Zeus out of trouble when he starts dreaming up wild adventures. Her quick and clever thinking helps settle arguments and solve problems. For instance, she figured out how to steer the *Argo*, a robot vacuum, which she now captains around the pet center. In the human world, she wears a gold collar with an owl charm, but the other Olympians see her wearing a laurel crown and two thin gold bracelets that wrap around her front paws.

Ares the pug is the strongest of the pet center Olympians. Courageous and impulsive like the god of war, Ares is the first to jump into an adventure and face any monster. But his excitement can sometimes get the better of him. (One time he accidentally sat on Poseidon's hose and almost suffocated the pufferfish!) Ares loves to be called a good boy and can eat an entire handful of Mutt Nuggets in one sitting, which probably contributes to his "meatloaf-ish" body. He wears a spiked collar and, among the Olympians, a bronze Spartan war helmet.

Poseidon is a white-spotted pufferfish that lives in the fish tank (known to the animals as the Aegean Sea) at Mount Olympus Pet Center. From his saltwater throne Poseidon rules over his fishy minions and challenges Zeus's authority over the center. The two regularly argue about who is the better ruler. Poseidon can leave his aquarium by swimming into a plastic diving helmet that has a long hose connected to the tank. He wears a tiny gold crown and carries a trident, just like the Greek god he's named after.

Artemis "Artie" Ambrosia is the owner of Mount Olympus Pet Center. In Greek mythology Artemis is the goddess of hunting and wild animals—so it makes sense that Artie has rescued the animals living at the center. It also makes sense that she named all her rescued animals after Greek gods, since she loves Greek mythology. She even listens to *Greeking Out,* a podcast that retells the famous myths and gives the animals crazy ideas for their adventures. Artie plans to open a rescue center next door to Mount Olympus so she can find *fur*-ever homes for more animals.

Hermes is the newest resident of Mount Olympus Pet Center. An Appenzeller hen (or lady chicken) who was rescued from a poultry ranch, Hermes misses her farm friends and hopes to find a new flock to join at the pet center. Ancient Greece is a new realm for Hermes, but that doesn't stop her from trying to live up to her name and become one of the Olympians. She'll need the courage of an Amazon to accomplish deeds worthy of Heracles and soar to new heights—not easy for a bird who can hardly fly.

ARTEMIS AMBROSIA CARRIED A BOWL OF
water through Mount Olympus Pet Center with the poise
of a tightrope walker. A tan pug danced at her feet,
threatening to throw her off-balance. "What, you think
I have Mutt Nuggets in this bowl, Ares?" she asked the
little dog.

At the mention of his favorite treat, Ares leapt against
the tall redheaded woman's shins. Water sloshed onto the
pug's wrinkly head. He yipped and ran off. "Serves you right,
goofball," Artemis chuckled. She continued to a new floor
fan near the aquarium section and unscrewed a cap on its
side. She poured the water into the fan, a special model
that sprayed a cooling mist. Nothing but the best for her
beasts to beat the heat now that summer had arrived in
Athens, Georgia.

Artemis—Artie for short—found Ares cowering behind
a display of leashes. She tossed him a Mutt Nugget from
her pocket. The pug snatched it from the air, swallowing it

in one slobbery gulp. "Still a little soggy, my ridiculous dog?" she asked him lovingly. "When did you become such a nuisance?" Artie glanced around Mount Olympus Pet Center to address the rest of her favorite rescued animals. "Same goes for all of you Olympians." She saw Athena the cat snoozing in her bed beneath the big picture window at the front of the center. Poseidon the pufferfish swam lazy laps around his aquarium, escorted by a school of seahorses as if they were his subjects in some underwater kingdom. Artie looked toward a shelf high above the cash register at the back of the pet center, where she spotted a familiar golden hamster snoozing in his bed of golden—fleece material. "You've all become legendary troublemakers!"

The animals ignored her, and Artie giggled. It's not like she expected them to answer for their recent misadventures: cats commandeering robot vacuums, rodents running amok. The truth was, a lot more happened in her pet center every night than she could ever imagine.

Artie walked toward the front door and turned off the light, plunging the room into the dim red glow of the Mount Olympus Pet Center sign in the front window. "Nighty night, Olympians. Everyone get some shut—eye!"

〜

CHAPTER 1

"**K**EEP YOUR EYES OPEN, OLYMPIANS,**" warned Zeus the Mighty as he crouched on the shore of the Aegean Sea. "The Hydra's close." The Olympians gathered together and huddled around their kneeling leader.

"Really?" Demeter the grasshopper peered about nervously, her eyes wide. The pillars of the Agora, meeting place of the Olympians, stood to the west. The coast of the Aegean Sea stretched from the north to the south. In the distance stood the rugged hills of Greece, crammed with their colorful relics and crates of goodies. Demeter saw no sign of a five-headed swamp monster. "What makes you think the Hydra's here?"

"This." Zeus dipped a finger into a puddle near his

knee. When he lifted it, slime dripped off his finger. "We're hot on its trail."

"That's … gross." Demeter scrunched up her face.

Ares the pug pushed his head past Demeter and sniffed the puddle, his wrinkly nose poking through the cheek guards of his Spartan war helmet. "I wouldn't drink that if I were you," he offered.

"Um, thanks," Demeter replied sarcastically. "I'll try to resist."

"No problem," Ares said with a goofy grin. "Happy to help."

"Let's keep moving!" hollered a pufferfish bobbing just offshore in the Aegean. "We have the Hydra in our grasp!" Before the Olympians could answer, the fish sped off to the north, his three-pronged crown cutting a wake like a shark's fin.

"You heard the sea lord. Poseidon's in charge today." Zeus stood up and tried to find something to wipe his slimy finger on. He reached out to clean it on Ares's fur, but the pug took off after the pufferfish.

"'Poseidon's in charge today,'" Athena repeated, shaking her head. The golden owl charm on her collar jingled. "Those are four words I never thought would come out of your mouth."

"What can I say?" Zeus shrugged. "We Olympians have had serious mojo lately. I like it." He reached out to wipe his finger on Demeter's back.

"Gotta go!" The grasshopper bounded out of reach.

"Mojo?" Athena repeated as she watched Demeter fall into step behind Ares. "You mean, like, we're not constantly arguing?"

"Right, we're getting along and doing our thing. You know, mojo!" Zeus lifted his finger slowly—then jabbed it toward Athena to wipe on her fur.

"Nope," Athena said as she leapt away from Zeus, twisted in midair, and landed at a trot behind Demeter, Ares, and Poseidon.

Zeus sighed and shook his finger to clean it as best he could, then hustled to follow the other Olympians north.

Soon they reached the spot where the Aegean coast curved to the east. Ares was waiting for them, nibbling at an itchy spot on his hind leg. Zeus saw Poseidon waving everyone closer. The land-based Olympians crept to the shore and watched the pufferfish expectantly.

"It's thataway," Poseidon hissed in a low voice. He pointed east along the shoreline with his trident.

Zeus and the Olympians craned their necks to see. Far off, barely visible in the early morning dimness, they could just make out a massive, scaly form hunched on the shore.

"You sure that's the Hydra?" Zeus squinted. "I don't see five heads."

"I don't see *any* heads," added Athena.

"Sure I'm sure," Poseidon said. "That creature has been camping on the shores of my realm every night for at least a week."

"Camping?" Athena repeated. "You mean it's just sleeping there?"

"That doesn't sound so bad," Ares said.

"You don't know these sea monsters like I do," Poseidon replied. "Today it's camping. Tomorrow it will be throwing a beach party with Scylla and Charybdis and the sirens. Next we'll be dealing with an entire sea-monster theme park."

"And ... that would be bad?" Ares asked, tilting his head.

"Yes, it would most certainly be bad," Poseidon answered firmly. "We need to convince the Hydra to leave while it's still on the beach. There'll be no getting rid of it once it slips into the water."

"So that's why you organized this hunting expedition!" Zeus exclaimed. "The Hydra is about to become your problem, and you want help while it's still everyone's problem."

Poseidon puffed up in protest, but Zeus raised his paws. "Relax, sea lord," Zeus said. "I agree, we should handle the Hydra together. We've been on a real winning streak lately."

"It's true. We found the Golden Fleece, and we defeated the Minotaur," Demeter said, counting off their achievements.

"Point is, we're a well-oiled machine—thanks to my amazing leadership skills." Zeus waited for the

Olympians to confirm this. They stared back blankly, so he moved on. "No reason to dial it back now." He began walking east toward the Hydra's hulking form. "Everyone take your places."

CHAPTER 2

"WAKE UP, SLEEPYHEADS!" ZEUS THE Mighty bellowed up at the five-headed monster snoozing on the shore of the Aegean Sea. "Nappy time's over!"

The Hydra didn't stir. Its heads hung limply at the end of long, scaly necks that sprouted from a stocky chest. Slimy drool dribbled from three of its five mouths into a puddle that reeked of low tide. A titanic helmet of iron bars encased the Hydra's heads in a sort of protective cage. Even hunched in sleep, the beast towered over Zeus, despite the hamster's best efforts to stand tall and puff out his chest beneath the fabric of his chiton.

Zeus noticed the ground was littered with crumbs of Mutt Nuggets, Ares's favorite snack. He picked up a morsel. "I said, wake up!" He chucked it at the Hydra.

It was a good throw. The Mutt Nugget struck the Hydra square in the chest, hitting what appeared to be a small crystal. The crystal lit up, and the Hydra swiveled slowly in Zeus's direction. It had awakened!

The five heads began whirling around its body, just short of scraping the inside of its strange iron helmet. The heads spun slowly at first, then faster and faster.

A breeze rippled the laurel-wreath crown on Zeus's head. "That's right—rise and shine!" he yelled.

The Hydra hissed, spitting mist. Its five necks kept whirling around and around within the helmet, kicking up a gale that blew a slobbery fog over Zeus.

"More like 'rise and slime,'" Zeus muttered as he wrinkled his nose and pushed damp fur from his eyes. His royal robes, as always, lay neat and dry. "Okay, we can either do this the

easy way or the hard way!" Zeus deepened his voice to sound intimidating.

"WAAAHHHHHH!" the Hydra bellowed in rage.

"Hard way it is!" Leaning into the wind, Zeus cupped his paws around his mouth. "Olympians, assemble!"

Athena leapt in front of Zeus, the gray hair on her back rose high in hackles. "Did you really think a multiheaded sea monster would choose the easy way?" she asked him.

"I don't much care." Zeus shrugged. "It sounded cool."

"Olympians assemble! Olympians assemble!" barked Ares as he barreled through Greece, his helmet teetering. He stopped in his tracks and sniffed at the crumbs on the ground. "Ooooh, Mutt Nuggets!"

Splish! The sea nearest the Hydra erupted in a spray of foam as Poseidon broke the surface. "The beach is closed today, foul creature!" he shouted, brandishing his trident.

From above, Demeter glided to a rough landing near the Hydra's scaly feet. She looked up at the monster, then covered the bottom of her face. "Ooof, talk about morning breath."

"Five heads make for five times the morning breath," said Athena.

Zeus kept his attention on the slimy giant. "Hydra, meet the Olympians!"

"Hi, Hydra!" Ares shouted cheerfully. His curly tail wiggled. The other Olympians maintained their fierce expressions.

"GAAAAHHHHHHH!" the Hydra bellowed in reply. Its spinning heads were a blur now inside their cage-like helmet, creating so much wind that Demeter was nearly lifted off her six legs.

"How come it doesn't get dizzy?" Ares asked.

"It has five heads but no brains," Athena said.

"No brains is good for us," Zeus said. "Stupid monsters are easy to defeat. Everybody ready?"

"The surf, as they say, is up!" Poseidon replied from the Aegean. Unconstrained by the dive helmet he used

to travel on land, the pufferfish had puffed up larger than the Olympians had ever seen him. He began bobbing on the surface, creating rippling waves that splashed over the dunes and soaked the Hydra's feet.

The monster's heads swiveled to the Aegean. It seemed momentarily mesmerized by the sea lord's mini tsunami.

"Remember, wait until the Hydra is completely distracted!" Demeter yelled, leaping to the far side of the five-headed beast.

"Right, then I'll go high," said Athena, preparing to pounce.

"I'll go … the opposite of high!" Ares called, aiming the brush-like top of his helmet at the Hydra's lower body.

"Just get that monster's necks in a knot, and I'll take it from there!" Zeus shouted.

"Not yet … not yet," Demeter cautioned, watching the Hydra's heads swivel. "Another second." The focus of all five heads was now on the pufferfish.

"Ready and—" Zeus was about to give the go-ahead, when, "Oooof!"

Zeus the Mighty's world turned black and white. He had been swallowed by what seemed like an endless cloud of dirty white fluff. It had come out of nowhere. "What … what is this?" He pressed against the white feathery mass, but his paws sunk into it. "*Aaaaachoooo!*" The stuff tickled his nose and poked into his mouth. It was like he was being crushed by a feather duster.

The only solid object he could find was the ground beneath him. So Zeus rolled until he could see the sky and was free from whatever had tried to smother him. He scrambled to his feet, certain that some new nightmarish beast had ambushed the Olympians while they were focused on the Hydra.

What he saw instead was the backside of a chicken. It was a female chicken—a hen—and she shuffled backward past Zeus as she scratched at the ground with her scaly talons, digging up the bits of Mutt Nuggets that were strewn about. Her plumage was white with black speckles. A wobbly mop of stubby feathers sprouted from atop her head while a rubbery red beard jiggled beneath her beak. She gobbled morsels with precise pecks. Zeus, Demeter, Athena, Ares, Poseidon, and even the Hydra all turned to stare at the chicken, who had so rudely interrupted this momentous moment.

The hen stopped her digging and gawked at the Olympians around her, as if noticing them for the first time. "Oh, hey, y'all," she said. "Am I interruptin' your little picnic?"

CHAPTER 3

"**D**OES IT LOOK LIKE WE'RE HAVING A picnic?" Zeus gestured at the Olympians, then pointed at the Hydra towering behind them.

The hen took in each Olympian, her crown of short feathers bobbing wildly, before peering up at the raging Hydra. She turned to Zeus. "Well, you oughta be." She waved a wing at the Mutt Nuggets. "This stuff's good eatin'!" She went back to pecking.

"I know, right?" Ares agreed excitedly. He bounded to the hen's side and slurped up a crumb.

"A lot better than what I'm used to," the hen mumbled with her beak full.

"Mutt Nuggets are best when they're fresh from the sack," Ares explained enthusiastically as he watched the chicken peck at the brown bits. "They just make this certain snap when you bite into 'em." He began to drool more than usual. "I mean, leftovers like these are still tasty and all, don't get me wrong ..."

The cloud-shaped patch of white fur on Zeus's cheek quivered as he watched Ares making small talk with the bird. No less than a minute ago, the Olympians had been working in sync, primed to twist the five-headed Hydra up in knots. Now their perfect plan was in tatters—their mojo was kaput—because of this chicken. And the hen didn't even seem to care. She just kept pecking away, shuffling backward until her fluffy butt was nearly bumping against the scaly body of the Hydra, which no longer seemed distracted by Poseidon's waves.

"Are we attacking this beast or what?" the overinflated pufferfish panted. "I can't stay this puffed up forever!"

Just as Zeus decided to take back control of the situation, a gray shape in the corner of his eye caught his attention. He turned in time to see Athena creeping low on her front legs, her rear stuck in the air. The white tip of her fluffy tail twitched. Her blue eyes were wide. Zeus noticed they had a wild look. "Um, Athena?" he asked. "What are you—"

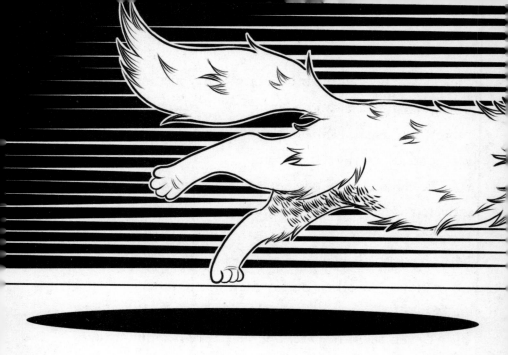

Suddenly, she was airborne, front claws aimed at the speckled hen pecking away obliviously at the Hydra's feet.

Ares was still explaining the finer points of Mutt Nuggets when he spotted Athena sailing above him. "Ooh, watch out, chicken!" Ares's warning came a moment before Athena would make contact. The hen leapt backward with a flurry of wings, just a feather's breadth from Athena's claws. Athena touched down lightly and immediately locked her eyes on the chicken. The cat sunk low, preparing for a second pounce, her tail twitching.

"Athena! What's gotten into you?!" Demeter shouted.

The cat shook her head and uncoiled her body. She peered around sheepishly, her eyes no longer wild, and saw Zeus, Demeter, Ares, and Poseidon staring at her, shocked.

"I … I don't know." Athena hung her head. "I saw that bird and just needed to pounce."

Ares turned left and right scanning for the hen. Finally, he found her sitting high above them on the Hydra's hunched back. The monster raged and hissed another cloud of icky vapor.

"Whoa! You're riding the Hydra!" Ares yelled up at the chicken. "Guys, the chicken is riding the Hydra!"

"Better get down from there!" Zeus shouted. "That beast will pluck you alive!!"

"This thing?" The hen stuck out a foot and jammed one of her talons through the wiry helmet that shielded the Hydra's heads. Her claw scraped against the monster's whirling necks with a *CLICK-CLICK-CLICK-CLICK*.

Their spinning slowed. The heads began raining drool instead of spitting mist.

"You are *fearless!*" Ares swooned. "Are you an Amazon?"

"No, I'm an Appenzeller," replied the hen, confused. "What's an Amazon?"

"They're, like, supertough birds," Ares explained. "Just like you! There's a whole flock of them in the northern lands—that's where I do my business." He nodded to the northwest. "You sure you're not an Amazon?"

"She's not an Amazon!" Zeus snapped, his cheek patch quivering in overdrive. He whirled on the hen above them. "Where'd you come from?"

She lifted her talon away from the Hydra's necks and pointed toward the other side of the Aegean Sea. "That nice human lady brought me here."

Five Hydra heads and five Olympian heads turned to look.

"Oh no!" Demeter cried. "Artie's here!"

CHAPTER 4

IT'S MORNING ALREADY?" ARES ASKED, noticing the sunlight streaming across Greece. "Time sure flies when you're fighting a stinky sea monster." The Hydra's heads were whirling at full speed again even with the chicken still perched on its scaly back. The beast had ceased hissing its foul fog.

"We would've vanquished the Hydra an hour ago if that pillow pile up there hadn't gotten in the way," Zeus said, glaring at the hen.

"Hey now!" The chicken folded her wings across her chest. "I was just mindin' my own beeswax until your feline friend tried to turn me into a scratching post." She nodded toward Athena.

The cat sunk to the ground and flattened her ears.

She looked like she was trying to disappear.

"Morning, critters!" called out a human voice. The animals turned to see a second woman, this one with sandy hair, entering Greece carrying a familiar green bag of tools.

"And now Callie's here, too!" Zeus threw up his paws and sighed. "That's just fantastic."

"I'll say," the hen said. "Now it's a party!"

"No, no!" Zeus growled. "I was being sarcastic, you silly goose."

"No, no, boss, that's a chicken," Ares offered helpfully.

"I KNOW SHE'S A CHICKEN!" Zeus's cheek twitching was unstoppable.

"Guys," Demeter said nervously, her eyes on the two humans across Greece, "we really need to get home before Artie catches us out."

PFFFFFTFF! In the Aegean Sea, Poseidon had deflated in a torrent of bubbles. "One of us is already home," the sea lord said. "If you'll excuse me, I must prepare my realm for the imminent invasion of the Hydra. Pity we couldn't stop it on land." The de-puffed pufferfish sunk into the Aegean Sea and swam toward his throne.

"Yeah, pity," Zeus repeated as he stared daggers at the

hen, but she didn't notice because Ares was chatting with her again.

"To be honest," Ares yelled up to her, "Mutt Nuggets are best when Artie heats 'em up ..."

Demeter still had her eyes on Artie and Callie, who were wandering in their direction. "We need a distraction, Zeus."

"War god," Zeus growled, cutting off Ares's Mutt Nugget monologue. "Will you be a good boy and go make a mess?"

"Ooh, I'm a good boy! I'm a good boy!" Ares barked and spun in a circle. He was about to take off but then glanced up at the hen perched on the Hydra's back. "Let's hang out later, chicken!" Ares turned and bolted straight onto the plains of Greece. Zeus, Athena, and Demeter waited.

Zeus started limbering up. "Get ready to make a run for it, gang."

Boom! Ares rammed his thick head into a stone column three times his height, knocking it over. Atop the column had sat a neat stack of moss-covered boulders, arranged days ago by Artie. The boulders crashed down, bouncing and rolling all over Greece. Ares scrambled over some of them, sending them in all directions. "Woo-hoo!" he hollered. "I'm a good boy! I'm a good—erk!"

A strong human arm wrapped around Ares's meatloaf body and pulled him into the air. "No! Bad Ares!" Callie said to the pug in her arms. He tucked his tail and whimpered. "Next time you want a tennis ball, just ask." Callie carried him across the pet center, careful to avoid stepping on the fuzzy green balls rolling underfoot.

Artie scrambled around displays and reached under shelves as she collected the scattered balls in the bottom of her T-shirt. "I can't believe my dog has *me* playing fetch," she muttered, glaring at Ares in Callie's arms. "Time for a time-out, puppers."

Callie nodded and locked Ares in his kennel.

The remaining Olympians hadn't had time to flee their hiding spot before Callie had scooped up Ares. Zeus could see Artie and Callie just south of the Aegean Sea, near Crete. They were still too close to make a break for home. "So much for Ares's distraction." He nodded at Athena. "You're up, goddess of wisdom. Go keep the people occupied."

"Why not?" She sounded resigned. "I don't quite feel like my brainy self, so I might as well go dance for the humans." She darted away, a blur of gray fur.

The moment Athena disappeared, the hen hopped off the Hydra's back and landed alongside Zeus and Demeter. "Anyone else feel safer now that the cat's gone?" The chicken shook out her wings. "So what do y'all do for fun around here besides ... whatever this is we're doing?" She waved around vaguely.

"I didn't send her away so we could chitchat," Zeus snapped.

"Then why'd you do it?" The hen sounded genuinely confused.

"You'll see," Demeter replied.

CHAPTER 5

CALLIE AND ARTIE WERE DEPOSITING THE scattered tennis balls in a box on a counter when a shrill beep echoed across Mount Olympus Pet Center. A low whirring followed, and then Athena appeared from behind the cash register riding atop a round blue machine.

"Classic distraction!" Demeter declared as Athena rolled by in the distance.

"What's that contraption?!" the chicken squawked, gawking.

"Works every time," Zeus said, ignoring her. "Get ready to make a break for Mount Olympus when Artie and Callie take the bait, Demeter."

Out on the plains of Greece, Athena sat at the helm of

the *Argo,* her paws dancing across the controls. *Beep!* She spun left. *Boop!* She turned right. "Watch me, Artie!" Athena yelled. "I learned some new maneuvers—hey!"

"Okay, not today, Athena." Artie pulled Athena from the deck of the machine, which continued running in a straight line without her captain. "You need to learn some new shenanigans." She carried the cat to a portal in the north below Mount Olympus. The door led to an airy land where the larger animals stretched their legs and went potty. Artie unceremoniously shoved Athena through the portal. "Go play outside for a while."

"So *this* is why my robot vacuum never has a full battery." Callie inspected the machine Athena had been riding and carried it to its recharging dock.

"What are we gonna do?" Demeter asked. "Artie's about two seconds from noticing you're not in your palace." She pointed a leg up at Mount Olympus, still maddeningly far away. "And then she will *freak!*"

"Maybe I can help you folks," the hen said.

Her suggestion surprised them. "How?" Zeus asked. "You going to fly us home?"

"We're trying to keep a low profile," Demeter added.

"Us flying home on a chicken's back is kinda the opposite of that."

"I'd carry you home if I could," replied the chicken, waving her wings, "but these things only get me so far."

"They got you up there, didn't they?" Zeus pointed up to the drooling Hydra.

The hen shrugged. "My wings are only good for a hop, skip, and a halfway decent jump—and even then I'm not too keen on heights."

Zeus didn't try hiding his frustration. "Let me get this straight: You're a bird who's afraid of heights and can barely fly," he said flatly.

"That about sums it up," the hen said. "So y'all are tryin' to get the human's attention, right?"

"That would literally be what a distraction is," Zeus said slowly, "so yes."

"Well, that I can do! Get a load of this!" The hen pumped her wings and awkwardly leapt onto the Hydra's back again. She cleared her throat and began belting out the worst tune Zeus and Demeter ever heard. "*Brach-crock-a-doodle-doooo!*"

Her song didn't seem to have a melody or even lyrics.

It sounded like someone with a sore throat screaming into a bottomless pit.

Zeus goggled at the hen, not believing what he was hearing. He drew his paw across his neck in a cutting motion. "Not low profile!" he hissed. "Definitely not low profile!"

Both Artie and Callie stopped what they were doing. "You have a rooster?" Callie asked, flabbergasted.

"Um, noooo," Artie said, "but I do have a hen now—a lady chicken. She's a new rescue I just brought in."

Callie cocked her head. "Your lady chicken sounds like a guy chicken."

"*Crock-a-doodle-do*!" The hen kept up her song even as the Hydra's heads writhed below her and Zeus waved frantically to stop.

But Demeter saw their opportunity. "Zeus, this is exactly the distraction we need!" She grabbed Zeus's paw and yanked him from their hiding spot. "Go, go, go! To Mount Olympus!"

"*Brach-crock-a-doodle-do*!" the hen continued.

Callie rounded the aquariums just as Zeus and Demeter dashed out of sight. She stopped. "Found your chicken," she called to Artie, who had walked up behind her.

Both women gawked at the hen roosting on the floor fan, which was switched to maximum and oscillating back and forth. Water dripped from the fan's center and pooled on the floor beneath it.

The chicken ceased crowing and cocked her head, inspecting the women with one eye, then the other, her crest of mini feathers bobbing.

"Settling in, my feathered friend?" Artie carefully looped an arm around the chicken and pulled her off the fan. The hen clucked softly in her arms. With her free hand, Artie reached down and switched off the fan. "That's funny—I don't remember turning this on when I left last night." She noticed the puddle at her feet. "Uh-oh, looks like the misting tank sprang a leak."

"You sure this isn't a rooster?" Callie was inspecting the hen.

"Two hundred percent," Artie said. "She used to be a bona fide egg-laying champ at the farm until she … wasn't. She was in line to receive the Kentucky-fried treatment."

"I take it that's why she's here now." Callie stroked the hen's neck and glanced away, noticing something on the tallest shelf in the pet center. "Well, your new performer here seems to have an audience," she said, chuckling. Callie pointed to the golden hamster standing at the bars of his habitat. He watched them intently.

"Aww," Artie cooed. "Does Zeus the Mighty like the newest addition to Mount Olympus Pet Center?" She held up the hen in her arms. The chicken let out a loud *be-kawk* when she made eye contact with the hamster.

"She certainly has a lot to say," Callie said. "What are you going to name her? I know it will be something from Greek mythology, but what?"

Artie regarded the chicken thoughtfully. "I think I have the perfect name."

CHAPTER 6

"I HAVE TO HAND IT TO THAT CHICKEN," said Demeter as she shut the gate in the back of Zeus's palace on Mount Olympus. "That singing was the perfect distraction!"

"Singing? Is that what that was?" Zeus ran a paw through the spiky fur atop his head. "Sounded more like the Minotaur with his head stuck in Poseidon's helmet." He was leaning against the pillars of his palace watching Artie and Callie while he caught his breath after their rapid return to Mount Olympus. "She did help us get home. I'll have to give her an autograph or something."

"I think she wants more than an autograph." Demeter took a nibble from the lettuce sash she wore around her shoulder. It was more than just her symbol as the harvest goddess; it was a portable snack to feed her bottomless bug appetite.

"Oh gods—you don't think she wants a Zeus action figure, do you?" Zeus ran to a small shelf. "I only have seventeen left!" He plucked one from the stack and held it out for Demeter to examine. "These things don't grow on trees!"

Demeter sighed as she inspected the object for probably the 10th time. It had a stick for a body, twigs for arms, and a crude lightning bolt carved into its chest. Zeus made them in his spare time from the bits of wood strewn among the material Artie spread across the floor of their palace. "They kinda do grow on trees, being wood and all," she said. "I wouldn't worry about running low."

"Are you kidding?!" Zeus swooned over his own figure. "These things are limited edition! They have ten points of articulation!" He bent the arm. *SNAP!* It came off in his paw. "Huh. Oops." He tossed the figure into a corner. "Sixteen left."

"I don't think that hen wants a souvenir," Demeter said, eager to get back on topic. "Zeus, she wants to hang out with us."

"*Her*, hang out with *us*?!" Zeus scoffed. "She can't! She's just a mortal. We're gods!" He looked out over Greece. "But the bigger deal is the effect she had on Athena. One glimpse of that chicken and she switched from brainy to beast mode! I've never seen her like that."

"Good point," Demeter agreed. "Hanging with us wouldn't be very good for that hen's health—or our sanity."

"Hear ye, hear ye," Artie announced down in Greece. "May I present the newest resident of Mount Olympus Pet Center." She held the hen in front of her and turned slowly so that everyone could see her. "Meet Hermes!"

"Um, howdy." Hermes waved a wing awkwardly.

The animals fell silent. The only sound in the center was the crickets chirping in the Bugcropolis.

"So why 'Hermes'?" asked Callie, hefting her bag of tools.

"Well, Hermes was the messenger of the gods," Artie said as she set the hen carefully on the ground, "not to mention the god of luck and sleep, and Hermes's symbol was a rooster." She watched the hen pecking the floor around her feet. "I don't know. The name just fits."

"Wasn't Hermes a guy god?" Callie nodded to the hen. "Hermes is a hen."

"A hen who crows like a rooster," Artie pointed out. "Just roll with it, all right?"

"Whatever you say." Callie shrugged. "As much as I'd like to stay and watch Hermes hang with your other gods and goddesses, I should get to work." Callie headed for the portal to uncharted territory. "See ya later!" she said before stepping through the portal and closing it behind her.

Artie started her morning routine tending Greece. Hermes followed as she filled food bowls and checked on the various residents. When Artie passed by Ares, still holed up in his chambers, the hen hung behind to watch the pug scarf down his breakfast.

"You say it's better when it's fresh from the sack, huh?" she asked, pointing a wing at his Mutt Nuggets.

Ares looked up, and his curly tail became a wiggly blur. "Hey, chicken!" he said excitedly, his wrinkled face breaking into a lopsided grin. Ares dashed to the door of his chambers so fast he slammed into it with his helmet. "So your name's Hermes, huh? That's a cool name."

"Now that you mention it," Hermes said, puffing out her chest, "it is a cool name."

"You hungry?" Ares darted back to his bowl and grabbed a mouthful of Mutt Nuggets, which he brought back and deposited in a slobbery pile before Hermes. "Dig in."

"Uh, thanks, but maybe later," Hermes said, eyeing the gooey morsels.

Ares returned to his bowl and resumed chowing down. "So, where are you going to live, anyway?" he asked.

"I dunno." Hermes shrugged. "Someplace with roommates would be nice, but I don't really know anybody here." Her wings slumped. "Back on the farm, I was part of a whole flock."

Ares's face lit up, and he froze mid-bite, then stood and spun in circles, spraying crumbs everywhere.

"What's up, pup?" Hermes backed out of the spray zone. "Get an extra juicy bit?"

"Better!" Ares stopped spinning and wobbled. "I got an idea! About your flock!"

"I don't follow." Hermes rubbed her rubbery beard.

"You just need to go talk to Zeus. He'll love my idea!"

"Zeus," Hermes repeated, crossing her wings. "Is he the fuzzy little fella or the cat who tried to eat me?"

"The cat's name is Athena, and I don't know what that was about. I've known her for years, and she's never tried to eat any of my other friends."

Hermes frowned. "That's not reassuring."

"Zeus is the boss," Ares said eagerly. "You go talk to him."

Hermes glanced at Mount Olympus in the north. "And what exactly do I tell him?"

CHAPTER 7

ZEUS'S MOUTH DROPPED OPEN AS HE STOOD at the pillars of his palace. "Say again?" he shouted down to the hen standing at the foot of Mount Olympus. "Did you just announce that you were joining the Olympians?"

"Yep, sign me up," Hermes called up to Zeus. "I'm your new messenger."

"That's ... swell," Zeus said, still gawking, "but what makes you think we need a messenger?"

Hermes was huddled along the mountain's western slope, next to the hidden rope that Zeus used to reach his palace. "This was Ares's idea. He said you'd be all over it."

"Oh, he did, did he?" Zeus sounded calm.

But Demeter knew better as she watched her best

friend. She could see the telltale twitching of Zeus's cloud patch from across the palace. "I told you the chicken wanted to hang out with us," she said in a hushed voice.

"So, um, it's Hermes, right?" Zeus yelled.

"That's my name." Hermes grinned. "Ask me again, and I'll say the same."

"Right." Zeus took a deep breath and smoothed the pristine fabric of his chiton. "The thing is, Hermes, we're not really accepting new members."

"That a fact? Why not?"

"I can think of a few reasons," Zeus replied curtly.

"Such as?" Hermes prodded.

"Well, for starters, from a practical standpoint, you pretty much turn Athena into a mindless vicious beast. I kinda need our goddess of wisdom to be, you know, wise. I'm sure you can understand?"

"I can't help it if your wisdom goddess has me confused with a can of cat chow." Hermes eyed the nearby portal to the northern lands, where Artie had dumped the cat earlier.

"But the bigger issue," Zeus pressed on, "is you have to be immortal to be an Olympian—a god. And you're …

well …" Zeus waved his hands vaguely.

"I'm what?" Hermes propped her wings on her hips.

"You're not a god. You're a bird who can hardly fly."

"Oh." Hermes cast her head down. "I reckon that's true. I mean, I am a bird—and a bird needs a flock." She looked around. "And you're telling me there's no flock for me here."

Zeus's spiky hair drooped as he felt a flush of pity. "Hold on." He grabbed an action figure from his shelf, then returned to the palace's western edge. "I appreciate how you helped Demeter and me get home this morning. That was a neat trick, that … song … thing you did. You deserve a reward." He held the figure over the ledge and dropped it. "Catch!"

Hermes reached out her wings and caught the figurine. She examined its rough features.

"You're lucky—that's handmade, limited edition!" Zeus shouted. "It's got ten points of articulation. There are only sixteen left!"

Behind Zeus, Demeter mouthed along to his description and rolled her eyes.

"Huh. Okay." Hermes tucked the figure under her

wing and cocked her head at Zeus. "Thanks ... I guess."

"Oh, my pleasure!" Zeus replied. "I mean, I wish I could help you with the other thing, but you can't just decide to become an Olympian. It doesn't work that way."

Hermes scratched at her floppy red beard for a moment. "Because I'm not a god?"

Familiar harp music drifted across the countryside, and Zeus suddenly wanted nothing more than to be done with this conversation. "Yeah, that's right."

"But if I became a god, then I could join you Olympians?"

"Uh-huh, whatever," Zeus said absentmindedly. Demeter shot Zeus a look, but he was scurrying to the front of his palace to watch Artie fiddling with the black rectangular device she carried with her everywhere.

The harp music got louder. Then it faded as a woman's voice began speaking: "Welcome to *Greeking Out,* your weekly podcast that delivers the goods on Greek gods and epic tales of triumphant heroes. I'm your host, the Oracle of Wi-Fi."

Zeus settled against a pillar to listen. He noticed that Hermes was moping off to the south, across the plains of Greece and back to Ares.

"This episode of *Greeking Out* is brought to you by Wingin' It Bird Treats," said the Oracle. "When you need to satisfy your feathered friends' need for seed, bring them some Wingin' It."

"Too bad Hermes can't join us Olympians," Demeter said, watching the hen retreat. "She was pretty brave against the Hydra."

"She's not immortal, so she can't be an Olympian," Zeus said curtly. "I don't make the rules."

"You don't? You're Zeus! You're king of the gods!"

"Pipe down! The Oracle's starting her lesson."

CHAPTER 8

"**T**oday's tale is about the most famous hero in Greece," the Oracle said.

"Well, well," Zeus brightened, "I knew it was only a matter of time before I got a lesson devoted to me."

Demeter sighed and hopped onto Zeus's Golden Fleece bed.

"This hero was courageous," the Oracle continued. "This hero was mighty."

Zeus beamed.

"He wasn't particularly smart," the Oracle said.

"Huh?" Zeus's shoulders slumped. Demeter stifled a giggle.

"His name was Heracles," the Oracle continued.

"Hairy-who?" Zeus asked.

"Hair-ah-*clees*," Demeter repeated.

"Heracles was the original action hero," the Oracle continued. "He was born with super strength and a knack for accomplishing heroic deeds. He even saved his twin brother from a snake in the crib. Some believe he had the blood of Zeus in him."

"He does sound like a chip off the old block." Zeus turned and saw Demeter nibbling on her sash. "You mind not getting green bits all over my Fleece?" he complained.

"But sometimes his powers got him into trouble," the teaching continued. "Heracles didn't know his own strength. He was always breaking things and accidentally hurting people."

"Sounds more like a chip off Ares's block," Demeter mused, picking lettuce pieces off the Fleece and popping them into her mouth.

"But what Heracles lacked in smarts, he made up for in heart and determination," the Oracle said. "He hated that his super strength caused problems and wanted to make up for his mistakes. So he visited the Oracle of Delphi—who was every bit as wise as your faithful Oracle of Wi-Fi. There, Heracles was told he could undo his misdeeds if he completed a set of challenges called labors."

"The labors of Heracles?" Demeter whispered. "Sounds exhausting."

"Pfft," Zeus scoffed. "Bet I could do them before lunch."

"And if he completed these labors," the Oracle explained, "not only would Heracles be forgiven—he would achieve immortality. He would become a god."

Zeus and Demeter locked eyes.

"A mortal becoming a god?" Zeus repeated. "Is that a thing?"

"It's a pretty big thing for you-know-who." Demeter looked worried.

"Who?" Zeus asked.

"Hermes."

"The chicken?" Zeus was lost. "Why?"

"Uh, because you told her she could become an Olympian if she was immortal," Demeter said.

"I did?" Concern crept across Zeus's face. "When?"

"Like, ten seconds ago!" Demeter shouted.

Zeus paused to think. "Blast it—I did!" He slapped his paw against his forehead. "I was just saying stuff to make her leave us alone."

"I don't think she'll leave us alone now," Demeter said.

"I bet she's going to try to do these labors of Heracles."

Zeus looked out over Greece with a worried expression. "Then we're just going to have to do them first."

CHAPTER 9

"**T**HAT ORACLE LADY, SHE KNOWS HER stuff?" Hermes asked Ares. The hen was back at the door of the war god's chambers, watching him scarf down the last of the Mutt Nuggets in his bowl.

"Oh yeah." Ares nodded, spraying crumbs. "She's a real know-it-all. Oh, hey, how'd it go at Mount Olympus? Did Zeus make you an official Olympian?"

"Eh, he made me *something,* but it ain't an Olympian." Hermes reached under her wing and touched the Zeus action figure she had stored there. "Sounds like I need to do a few things first."

"Really?" Ares cocked his head. "What kind of things?"

"**For one of his first labors,**" the Oracle said, continuing her lesson, "Heracles had to slay the Hydra, a fearsome five-headed swamp monster."

"That kinda thing," Hermes said, cocking an ear toward the Oracle's voice. "The labor thing that the lady's talking about."

"Ah, that makes sense," Ares said. He'd trotted back to his bowl. "The Oracle's always givin' us hints and stuff about our next big adventure."

"The Hydra was a most formidable opponent," the Oracle continued. "No matter how quickly Heracles could lop off its heads, the creature regrew them."

"Ain't the Hydra that thing you Olympians were playin' with this morning?" Hermes asked. The war god was busy sniffing around his bowl, oblivious to the Oracle's teachings.

"But once Heracles accepted a challenge, he refused to quit. He finally defeated the Hydra through pure perseverance. He'd completed one labor, with many to go. Next, he had to

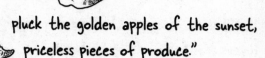

pluck the golden apples of the sunset, priceless pieces of produce."

"Sounds simple enough," Hermes said. "You learn a lot about produce livin' on a farm."

"Finding the apples wasn't a simple task," the Oracle explained, as if she'd heard Hermes. "They grew only in a secret garden in some northern land, under guard by the Hesperides, triplet sisters of the evening."

Hermes peered all around. "Northern lands, huh? Where are they?"

Ares waved vaguely toward Mount Olympus. "Thataway. That's where Athena and I go out to play."

"And for the next labor," the Oracle continued, "Heracles had to claim the belt of Hippolyta."

"Hippoli-who?" Hermes repeated awkwardly.

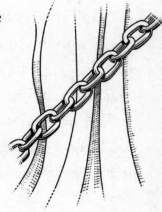

"Hip-ah-lit-ah," Ares answered. "She's the queen of the Amazons."

"Amazons? Now where have I heard that word before?" Hermes's eyes grew distant as she racked her brain. "Wait a minute! Ares, didn't you ask if I was an Amazon when ya met me?"

"Huh? Oh yeah." The pug had settled onto his bed. "They're good buddies of mine. They're out in the northern lands, too, way up high in the east. I'll introduce you sometime—Oh, hi, Athena!"

"Athena?!" Hermes whirled around to see the cat already in the air, claws out, heading straight for her.

CHAPTER 10

N MOUNT OLYMPUS, ZEUS LOUNGED IN
his exercise wheel and pondered the Oracle's
lesson, which Artie had stopped for the day.
"These labors of Hairy-clees don't sound all that
laborious," he said.

"I might agree if we had actually defeated ol' morning
breath earlier." Demeter sipped from the water bottle on
the wall. "Last I saw, the Hydra was alive and spitting."

"Whose fault was that?" Zeus bolted upright.

"*Bra-kawww!*" Hermes squawked in the distance as
if in answer to his question. Her call was followed by
a bloodcurdling hiss that brought Zeus and Demeter
to the palace's edge. Hermes was scrambling below,
her wings held wide, as if she were trying to take flight.

Hot on her tail was Athena, claws out. Just as Athena pounced, the hen squawked another *bra-kawww* and pumped her wings, which propelled her out of claw's reach. Athena landed and rolled, tumbling through the Agora, sending its rope-wrapped pillars toppling. She hissed again and scampered after Hermes.

Up on Mount Olympus, Zeus and Demeter watched helplessly. "What in blazes is wrong with that cat?" Zeus asked.

"Athena!" Artie had raced over from Poseidon's realm, where she'd been scraping algae off the sides of his sea. Hermes dashed between her legs, and when Athena tried to follow, Artie scooched her feet together, trapping the cat. She picked up a squirming Athena with both hands. "Since when did you become such a wild animal?"

Athena's eyes lost their crazed look. She went limp in Artie's arms.

"What's all the ruckus?" Callie stood in the door to uncharted territory. "Sounds like a real circus is happening in here."

"More or less," Artie said as she carried Athena toward the kennels at the front of the store. "I guess I should've known better than to let a bird be free-range anywhere near the shop cat—at least not before they got acclimated to each other." She reached down and opened Ares's crate. "Time-out's done, meatloaf," she said to the pug as he scampered to freedom so quickly, his feet slid on the smooth floor. "Now it's kitty's turn in the penalty box." She set Athena in Ares's place and closed the crate's door.

"Maybe Hermes can roost out back?" Callie suggested. She bent down and carefully scooped up the hen, who had been huddling near her feet.

"That's actually not a bad idea," Artie agreed, "at least until Athena can overcome her cat instincts. The apple tree will be the perfect roosting spot for her. I'll get the doggy door for you." Artie headed over and pushed open the dog-size portal that the larger animals used to access the airy northern lands. Callie pushed Hermes through it.

A new trio of humans entered Greece through its main portal just then, and Artie attended to their needs, which she so often did. Callie strolled to the eastern edge of the Aegean and began fiddling with something.

Zeus paid her no attention. Far to the south, he could see Athena hunched in Ares's chambers, her head sunk low. Ares moseyed to Athena's bed and plopped down for his nap. The two Olympians had traded places.

CHAPTER 11

ZEUS WATCHED ATHENA FOR A LONG WHILE, hoping she would snap out of it. Athena was one of the most formidable Olympians, and she was a good friend. Zeus retreated into his palace and nibbled on a piece of Fuzzy Feast, but he didn't have much of an appetite. He took a drink from his water bottle, and then hopped atop the Golden Fleece. Eventually, he fell asleep while trying to think of a way to help Athena.

The shadows had grown long over Greece when Demeter's urgent voice awakened Zeus. "Come quick!" she cried. "Callie's doing something with the Hydra!"

Zeus stumbled groggily to the palace's edge and was shocked to see Callie carrying the monster in her arms. All five of its heads were still and silent—either asleep or playing dead. Slimy drool dribbled from several of its slack mouths. Ares followed along at her feet, leaping against her legs and trying to nip the monster.

"Good boy, Ares!" Zeus yelled. "Don't let that beast get away!"

"Bad boy," Callie said. "The fan is not a chew toy."

"Taking the fan for a walk?" Artie joked as she paused from restocking a display of leashes.

"I'm putting it someplace where these furry goofballs can't get to it tonight," Callie said.

"Good idea!" Artie exclaimed. "No point in taking any chances after today's nonsense." She scowled at the animals.

"I'll patch up the mist tank and find a place to install it tomorrow where it's out of reach," Callie said. Zeus watched her carry the Hydra through the portal to uncharted territory.

"Oh, great," Zeus groused. "Not only do we have to tackle the Hydra from scratch—we have to track it all over again, too!"

"There's also the two other labors: the golden apples and the Amazon's belt," Demeter said. "Maybe we can focus on them first?" She watched Callie return from uncharted territory without the Hydra but carrying her green bag.

"Good thinking," Zeus said as he cast his gaze over to Ares's chambers. Athena was still hunkered in the same spot, moping. "I guess it doesn't matter what order we complete them in as long as we do them before that chicken."

"Seems like Artie and Callie are heading out for the evening," Demeter said.

Callie was standing by the main portal to Greece, and Artie was wrapping up her evening routine, securing the roof of the Bugcropolis and switching off the magical sunlight. Now Greece was plunged into the red glow of the Mount Olympus Pet Center sign. "Nighty night, Olympians," Callie said as she opened the portal.

"I'd tell you to stay out of trouble, but what's the point?" Artie said, turning to leave. She turned back at the last second. "But I'm going to do it anyway. Especially you, Athena and Ares!" she said to the cat and dog. "You're both in the doghouse!" She closed the door and locked it.

Zeus wasted no time. "Olympians, assemble!" he called

through the pillars of his palace. He watched his crew scramble toward the meeting place—all except one. Athena still sulked in Ares's chambers far to the south.

"C'mon, Athena," Zeus muttered. "Snap out of it."

"You think she can't open Ares's door?" offered Demeter. She had also been watching Athena.

Zeus scoffed. "Oh, please. You think the captain of the *Argo* can't open a door?"

"Sorry," Demeter muttered. "I'm just as worried about her as you are, buddy."

Zeus ran a paw through the fur atop his head. "All right, time to do what I do best."

"You're gonna make more action figures?"

"No! I'll go break our goddess of wisdom out of her chicken-fried funk." Zeus stood tall. "Demeter, you head to the Agora and get everyone hyped for the labors. We're going to knock these off so quick, people will ask 'Hairy-clees who?'"

"Okay!" The grasshopper squeezed through the pillars and leapt into thin air. She unfolded her tiny wings and glided to the rugged landscape far below. Zeus slid down the rope to the floor of Greece and raced south to Ares's chambers as fast as his feet could carry him.

CHAPTER 12

ZEUS SKIDDED TO A HALT IN FRONT OF Ares's chambers, out of breath but determined to motivate Athena. The cat hadn't moved in the slightest. Her face was buried in her paws.

"What's up, pussycat?" Zeus asked. "I summoned you to assemble. Didn't you hear me?"

"Yes," Athena said.

"So are you assembling or what?"

"No."

"No?" Zeus walked to the gate and examined its locking mechanism. "What, you telling me you can't figure out how to open a door?"

"No." Athena didn't move.

Zeus was getting frustrated. He stood on his tippy-toes

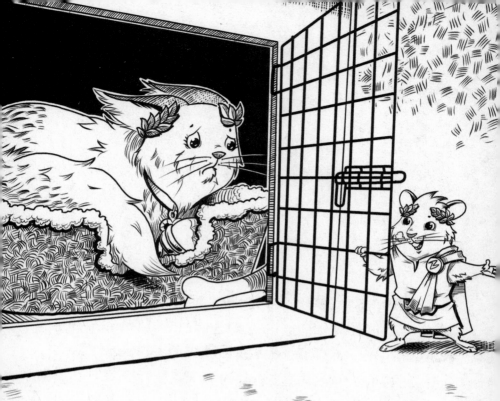

and unlatched the door, then slowly pulled it open,
grunting with the effort. "You're freeeeee!" he exclaimed
once he had the gate wide open.

Without looking up, Athena reached out a paw
and yanked the gate from Zeus's grip, pulling it shut.
"Better keep that closed tight, King," she said, her voice
muffled. "Don't you know I'm a wild animal?"

Zeus stomped forward and yanked the gate open
again. "Athena!" he shouted. "You get out of Ares's house
right now!"

She still didn't budge. Zeus took a deep breath and smoothed his royal robes. "If this is about that blasted chicken bringing out your wild side, quit worrying. Artie banished her to the northern lands."

Athena's ears perked up, and she lifted her head. "She did?"

Zeus nodded.

"Why didn't you say so?" Athena hopped to her feet and strolled casually past Zeus toward the Agora. "Ares's place smells like pug butt."

Zeus poked his nose into Ares's chambers and took a whiff. "Yep," he said, wrinkling his nose. "Pug butt."

He turned and scrambled to catch up with Athena. "So, uh," he stammered as he strolled alongside her, "what exactly is the deal with you and Hermes?"

"You mean, why am I trying to eat her?" Athena stared straight ahead as they walked.

"Good place to start." Zeus sidestepped one of the fuzzy green boulders Ares had spilled across Greece.

"What can I say? She brings out my worst instincts," Athena explained. "It's a cat-and-bird thing. It's not complicated."

Zeus could tell Athena was still sulking, but he decided to ignore it. "Then solving this isn't complicated, either. We'll just stay far, far away from that bird. She was getting under my skin anyway, and ... now what?" Zeus noticed that Athena had suddenly stopped, her hackles raised. She was focused on something over his shoulder.

He whirled around and gasped.

A fearsome feline creature with a raggedy golden mane crouched near a boulder, watching them coldly. It was preparing to pounce.

CHAPTER 13

"**N**OW *THAT*," ZEUS WHISPERED, "IS A wild animal."

"Yep," Athena whispered back. She had sunk to the floor behind one of the green boulders and was watching the strange, crouching beast. "Oh, this guy is good," she muttered. "Hasn't moved a muscle."

Zeus backed up until he bumped into Athena's front paw and almost sat on it. The lion wasn't imposing in size—it was a mere kitten as far as big cats went, smaller than Athena—but it hadn't blinked once while it stared at them. Was it hungry?

"Why's this lion giving us the stink eye?" Zeus puffed out his chest and tried to match the lion's gaze. "Doesn't he know who we are?"

Athena took her eyes off the lion to examine their surroundings. "I know this place. We're in Nemea. It's famous for one thing."

"Let me guess: a bloodthirsty lion?" Zeus asked.

Athena shook her head. "The Nemean lion isn't bloodthirsty—it's indestructible."

"If he's so tough, how come I've never heard of him?" Zeus asked loudly, not caring if the lion overheard. "Indestructible, huh? Gosh, it's just too bad we aren't, like, immortal gods with fabulous powers, for crying out loud!" Zeus pounded his chest. He kicked the green boulder at their feet and sent it rolling toward the lion's hiding spot. "Yowch!" The boulder turned out to be a lot harder than he expected. He hopped on one foot and rubbed his sore toe.

"Shush!" Athena hissed, and Zeus stopped hopping. Both Olympians held their breath as the fuzzy boulder rolled slowly, *slooowly* toward the lion. The beast maintained its rock-still pose. It hadn't even blinked.

"Huh." Athena gently pushed Zeus out of the way as she scooched toward the lion. "Something is off about this guy."

"Yeah, I'll say," Zeus said. "He's playing tough with two Olympians."

"No," Athena said, sniffing at the lion. "He's not playing anything." She walked right up and used one paw to whack aside the boulder in front of the lion. With her other paw, she whacked the lion himself. *SQUEAK!* It tumbled over, sprawling in a furry heap.

Zeus eagerly crept closer. He could see the lion wasn't breathing. He stood over it, then used his sore toe to nudge it gingerly. The lion let out a longer *SQUEEEAAK.*

"That's the most pathetic roar I've ever heard." Zeus rubbed the lion's coarse fur. His paw brushed a flap of fabric imprinted with an image of a bone above a strange script.

Dog-Nab-It Squeaky Toys
Leon the Lion
STUFFLESS · HYPOALLERGENIC

Athena gave Zeus a giant grin. "The Nemean lion might have been indestructible, but he wasn't immortal. This is his hide!" She took in the rugged terrain around them. "It must have been dislodged by Ares's antics. Came down from some cave or vault up there."

"Okay, cool." Zeus had already lost interest and was walking away.

"Don't you get it, King?" Athena said. "This is an incredibly potent relic! It's right up there with your aegis shield and Hekate's torch!"

Zeus turned back. "Really? Do tell!"

"Whoever wears the hide of the Nemean lion is imbued with his powers. In other words, you'd be indestructible!"

Now Zeus was excited. He lifted the hide and swung it around his shoulders. The lion's mane settled over his head like a hood, with its face and whiskers resting above Zeus's brow. "How do I look?"

Instead of answering, Athena raked her claws down the side of the Nemean cloak.

"HEY!" Zeus winced, then relaxed as he inspected his side. "Heyyy." He was unharmed. "You're a genius, Athena! With this relic on our side, we'll check off Hairy-clees's labors so fast that everyone will ask 'Hairy-who?'"

Athena did a double take. "We're doing the challenges from the Oracle's lesson?"

"Well, yeah," Zeus said as if it were obvious. "We gotta do them before that hen does. Otherwise she'll become immortal, and if she becomes

immortal, she'll join us Olympians. And if she joins us, you'll be stuck in this mopey beast mode of yours forever."

"Wait, wait, back up here." Athena raised a paw, her golden bracelet glinting in the light. "I know I've been off my game lately, but where did Hermes get the idea she could join the Olympians if she became immortal? The Oracle didn't say that."

Zeus cast his gaze down to his lion cloak and brushed absentmindedly at a rough spot on its fur. "Gosh, beats me," he said in a small voice.

"Zeus," Athena said sternly, "you can't fool the biggest brain in Greece. Come clean."

"Okay, I might've kinda told Hermes she could join us if she becomes immortal," Zeus blurted. "Let's get going." Without waiting for Athena's reply, he dashed north to the Agora. Stunned, Athena watched the mangy tail of his Nemean cloak drag on the ground behind him. Eventually, she padded along in Zeus's wake.

CHAPTER 14

ZEUS AND ATHENA SPRINTED TO THE Agora. Zeus slowed to a halt and turned in a circle, his new lion cloak flaring out around him.

"Demeter?" Zeus called. "Ares? Poseidon?" No one answered. He turned to Athena. "Where is everyone?"

Athena gave Zeus an icy stare.

He raised his paws. "I'll admit I never should've told that chicken she could join us if she became immortal."

"Her name's Hermes," Athena replied. "You should at least use her name since you practically invited her to join our team."

"I didn't, but whatever." Zeus pressed on. "It won't matter if we just do Hairy-clees's challenges before Hermes gets a chance. Now help me find everybody, will ya?"

Athena glared at him a moment longer, then sniffed around the pillars of the Agora. She stopped to scratch at one of them with her two front legs. When her paws reached the bottom of the pillar, she froze. "Well, they *were* here. Then they headed that way." She nodded to the west.

Zeus tried to peer west, but his lion's mane hung over his eyes. He pushed the hood back on his head. "How do you know that's where they went?"

"Follow the hose." Athena held up a skinny black hose—Poseidon's lifeline. It trailed behind him wherever he traveled on land. Now the hose snaked through the Agora and off into the plains to the west. "Assuming the sea lord is with the other Olympians," Athena said, setting off to follow the hose, "we'll find them all at the end of this line."

Zeus pulled the lion's mane back onto his head. "Good to see you using the old noodle again, Athena." He set off west after her.

Soon they reached the end of the lifeline. It snaked up and through the dog-size portal on the northern edge of Greece, just west of Mount Olympus. "Oh, great,"

Zeus muttered. "They went through there."

"Why'd they go to the northern lands?" Athena sounded mystified.

"Who knows. All I know is you-know-who is out there."

"The chicken," Athena whispered.

"I'm going through." Zeus spit on his paws and rubbed them together, then gripped Poseidon's lifeline. "You stay here."

"What?! Why?!" Athena argued. "The northern lands are my lands, too!"

"You know why. That chicken—Hermes," Zeus added the name hastily, "doesn't exactly bring out your best side." Zeus started climbing up Poseidon's lifeline paw over paw, using his feet against the portal for support. When he reached the point where the lifeline snaked through the portal, Zeus turned to look at Athena. "Uh, a little help?"

"Fine. Just bring the Olympians back ASAP." Athena reached out and pushed open the portal.

"That's the plan." Zeus flung himself over the edge. "Be back in a jiff." He disappeared from view.

CHAPTER 15

ZEUS HAD RARELY VISITED THE NORTHERN lands. It was indeed airy—even a bit chilly. And while much of the landscape was lost in the early evening shadows, he could make out strange terrain and unfamiliar landmarks.

The ground beneath his feet felt like smooth stone, though it ended not far to the north in a field of scrubby grass dully lit by the last rays of the sun. To the east he could see curious structures built from wood. They resembled hurdles, platforms, and ramps. "And I thought uncharted territory was strange," Zeus wondered aloud.

"Zeus?" Demeter's voice was close by. "Zeus! What are you wearing?!" She was suddenly standing before him, inspecting him from head to toe.

"Demeter," Zeus said sternly, "where is everyone?" He tried to see past the grasshopper, but she was in his face.

"What a cool lion outfit!" she said. "Where'd you get this?" She reached out and tapped at a small bump on its back and the cloak let out a soft squeak. "Ho!" Demeter giggled. "What was *that*?"

"Later, later." Zeus waved her away. "I need to talk to the other Olympians." Demeter hopped backward, which allowed Zeus to see Poseidon floating in his dive helmet next to Ares. Before them stood Hermes the hen. She appeared to be holding court among his Olympians. Zeus's cheek patch was in a tizzy. "What in blazes is going on out here?!" Zeus demanded.

"Good evening, Zeus!" Poseidon said cheerily. "My, but that's an interesting outfit!"

"Oh, wow! I'll say!" Ares bounded over and lunged at Zeus with his snout, ready to lick his lion cloak from mane to tail.

"No, no, no, no! Bad god!" Zeus shoved away Ares's tongue and immediately regretted it, shaking slobber off his paws.

Ares was unfazed by the scolding. "You're just in time,

boss!" He spun around and dashed back to Hermes.

"Just in time for what?" Zeus wiped his paws on the sides of his cloak.

"To watch me do the first of that Hairy-clees fella's labors," Hermes answered. She eyed Zeus. "Fancy duds."

Zeus shook the lion's mane off his head and rounded on the Olympians. "You all ignored my summons for this?!" he roared.

"I was just following him." Demeter pointed at Poseidon.

Poseidon froze in his helmet. "And I was just following him!" He pointed his trident at Ares.

Ares appeared perplexed. "I thought Hermes doing these labor thingies was all your idea, boss."

"It was absolutely most definitely NOT MY IDEA!" Zeus shouted.

The animals all fell silent. Hermes began quietly edging away from the group.

"Well, this is awkward," said Poseidon. He inspected his trident and buffed one of the tines with a fin. A chill breeze scattered a few leaves around them, but otherwise it was silent.

"What's the problem, boss?" Ares tilted his head. "Hermes'll make a good Olympian. She can fly."

Zeus crossed his arms. "That's a stretch."

"She's fearless," Ares countered.

"And we're not?" Zeus raged. "I mean, I can't count the number of times we've bravely faced being drowned, stepped on, eaten by a dragon, roasted by a Minotaur—and that's in just the last month alone!"

"Five times," Demeter offered helpfully. "It was two times for drowning, and—"

Zeus cut her off. "Five times we've charged into the face of certain death!" Zeus repeated. "I'd say we're pretty fearless!"

"True, true," Poseidon chimed in, glancing up from his trident, "but wouldn't having another Olympian on hand perhaps help in those situations? Especially one as capable as that Heracles fellow from the Oracle's tale?"

"It's not that simple, sea lord," Zeus snapped. "Hermes is bad for our mojo."

"I don't know about that, boss." Ares tilted his head.

"You doubt your king?" Zeus snapped.

"No, I mean I don't know about that word you just used."

"Athena." Zeus, frustrated, threw up his paws. "I'm talking about Athena. She loses her cool when Hermes is around. And her losing control throws off our team dynamic. Our *mojo*."

"Not my fault," Hermes chimed in from a distance.

Demeter turned to see why the hen sounded so far away. "Umm, guys?" she said, alarmed.

Zeus spun around, irritated. "Wha—" He clammed up when he saw what Demeter was worrying about. Hermes had wandered north and was standing at the edge of the grassy field.

The hen was staring at something. Zeus looked into the gloom and made out a large shape. Its top half was ablaze in the rays of the sunset. Zeus saw leaves and branches and a single golden apple near the top.

"The golden apple of the sunset, I presume," Poseidon said.

"One of Heracles's labors," Demeter added.

"Okay, Olympians." Zeus clapped his paws. "We gotta get that apple."

"Not if I get it first," Hermes called.

Ares glanced between Hermes and Zeus, then up at the apple. "How we gonna get it anyway, boss? Athena's the only Olympian who can climb that high, and she's not here."

Suddenly, three figures materialized in the branches just beneath the apple. They were hunched menacingly on rodent-like hind legs. One figure stood slightly in front of the others and revealed a ghastly smile of yellow fangs. All three were tethered to the tree's branches with bushy tails that seemed rimmed in blazing flame. In fact, their bodies appeared sheathed in fire instead of fur. Only their eyes were dark: pits of jet black.

"If you dare touch the apple!" shouted the lead figure in a deep, clear female voice.

"With our flames you shall grapple!" shouted the figure to her left.

The figure on the right opened her toothy mouth, then closed it. The other two watched expectantly. Finally, she stammered, "W-w-we're always r-r-ready ... for a ... scrapple?" She shrugged apologetically.

All three figures reared back their heads and screeched into the evening sky.

CHAPTER 16

HERMES STOOD AT THE FOOT OF THE enchanted tree peering up at the three fiery figures. "Hey, Ares, you know these jokers?" she asked without taking her eyes off them.

"Never seen them before," Ares replied, "but then, I've never been out here this late."

"They're obviously the guardians of the apple that the Oracle spoke of," Poseidon said. "The triplet sisters of the evening."

"Them we be!" shouted the lead figure.

"We're the Hesperides!" added the second.

"The Hesperides ... are ... us?" the third figure finished uncertainly. The leader shook her head.

"Aww. It seems like that last one must have stage

fright or something," Ares said, tilting his head sympathetically.

The other Olympians noticed the shadows creeping higher on the enchanted tree. Soon the blazing upper branches would be lost to the sunset.

And, Zeus realized, so would the golden apple! His spirits lifted. If he couldn't get the apple, neither could Hermes. She would fail at Hairy-clees's labors before she even started.

Hermes had seen the growing shadows, too, and frantically searched for a way to reach the apple. She saw none.

The Hesperides noted her panicked glances.

"Our defenses, you won't beat," the lead figure taunted.

"Flee now; you can't take the heat!" shouted the second figure.

The third figure's fiery face was scrunched up in concentration. Everyone waited.

"Let's all get something to eat," Ares suggested.

The Olympians stared at him. "What?" he said sheepishly. "I was just trying to be helpful."

Hermes called up to the tree, "Instead of tryin' to

rhyme or whatever, how about you just chuck me that apple and we'll call it a day?"

The Hesperides hissed, and their flaming fur flared twice as bright.

"Oh, they didn't like that," Demeter muttered.

Hermes, to her credit, remained unfazed.

Zeus paid little attention to the flaming figures. He was busy trying to will the sun to set faster and steal the apple from Hermes's grasp.

While everyone focused on the tree, a dark shape slipped silently past them—until the glint of a golden owl charm caught Zeus's eye. "Athena?! I told you not to follow me into the northern lands!"

Her cover blown, Athena pounced. Zeus had provided just enough warning for Hermes to flap herself out of the way. But the hunt was on again. Hermes quickly headed south, toward the odd wooden structures barely visible in the deepening shadows.

CHAPTER 17

"**A**THENA! WOULD YOU PLEASE COME TO your senses!" yelled Poseidon.

"It's like we don't even know her anymore," Demeter added.

High above, the Hesperides seemed amused by this turn of events. "Things have taken a turn for the absurd," observed the leader.

"Who truly seeks the apple: cat or bird?" asked the second.

The third figure hunched quietly, clearly struggling.

Ares yelled up at her: "Don't overthink it! Just say the first thing that pops into your head!"

Athena ignored them all. She had the wild look in her eyes as she jigged and bobbed to stay on Hermes's tail.

Hermes reached the first wooden structure: a ramp that overlooked a chasm, with a corresponding ramp far on the other side. Sprinting to stay ahead of Athena, Hermes leapt off the ramp, stuck out her wings for a brief gliding flight, and landed deftly on the other ramp. She didn't need to check to know that Athena had also easily bridged the gap. She could hear the cat's claws scraping the ground behind her.

"Woo-hoo!" Ares stood on his hind legs and clapped his front paws. "Good air, Hermes! Good air! Ooh—watch out for the hurdles!"

"Hurdles?" Zeus pushed the lion's mane hood out of his eyes and stood on tiptoe to try to see the chase, but he

was too low to the ground and Athena and Hermes were too far away. He scrambled to Ares's side. "War god, give your king a lift!"

"You got it, boss." Ares bent his front legs while Zeus grabbed one of the spikes on the pug's collar and swung up onto his back. He braced himself behind Ares's helmet, parting the bristles of its brushy plume for a better view. From this vantage, he could see it all. The chase had taken Athena and Hermes through a series of hurdles. Hermes cleared the last one just inches ahead of Athena, only to land on a large platform that skidded forward on hidden

wheels. When it came to an abrupt halt, Hermes flung herself off and continued forward at top speed.

"Nice dismount, Hermes!" Ares yelled.

"What in blazes is all that junk they're running through?" Zeus asked.

"Callie built that stuff for me," Ares answered proudly. "She calls it my doggy obstacle course, so I can stay a strong god of war." He flexed his chest. "It's like the best thing ever!"

"No wonder you like Callie so much," Zeus muttered.

"Obstacle course?" Poseidon asked from the ground next to them. The pufferfish was swimming as high in his dive helmet as he could, his face pressed against its clear surface. He held his fins like binoculars in front of his oversize eyes. "I can't see a thing."

"I'll give you a boost, too!" Ares grabbed Poseidon's helmet by its lifeline and lifted his head, jerking the helmet six inches into the air.

"Whoooa! Easy!" Poseidon righted himself in the churning water as his helmet hung upside down from Ares's wrinkly mouth. Drips of slobber rained on the clear surface. "Hey, mind the drool!"

"Thorry," Ares said around the mouthful of lifeline.

"I need a boost, too," Demeter said. She hopped up next to Zeus and watched the action, transfixed, as she nibbled on her lettuce sash.

The Olympians all saw that the chase wouldn't last for long. Hermes had headed for a dead end. She had nowhere to run except across the final obstacle, a narrow board supported at its middle by a rocky mound. "The teeter-totter!" Ares managed to mumble around Poseidon's lifeline. "Oh, that ith thuch a fun one!"

Hermes hopped on the tip of the narrow board and turned to face Athena. The cat dug her claws into the ground and came to a halt. The two animals eyed each other. Athena knew she had Hermes now. Hermes had no place to go but up the narrow board, to the high side of the teeter-totter.

The hen risked a glance up and saw the shadows of sunset had nearly consumed the enchanted apple tree. A cool breeze rippled through its gloomy lower branches. Only the golden apple at its very top and the Hesperides just below it were ablaze in the last rays of sunlight. In less than a minute, they, too, would disappear.

All three Hesperides were watching the action with their odd jet-black eyes.

"Our day soon comes to an end," called the leader.

"Not unlike a certain hen," added the second.

"Never to be seen again!" the third figure shouted triumphantly.

After a brief pause, the other Hesperides threw back their heads and cheered.

"Thee, ith not tho hard!" Ares yelled encouragingly around Poseidon's lifeline.

Seeing the chicken distracted, Athena leapt. But Hermes scooched up, over the board's midpoint to the teeter-totter's high side, which began falling under her weight. Athena landed where Hermes had been only a

moment ago, plunging the
teeter-totter down—and
catapulting Hermes
skyward! She soared
above Athena, heading
in the direction of the
enchanted tree.

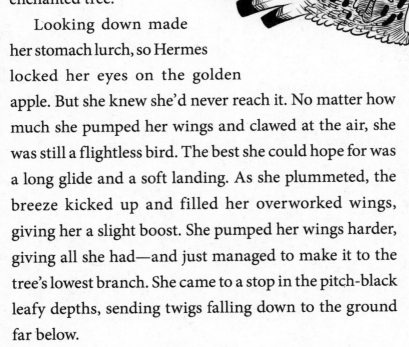

Looking down made
her stomach lurch, so Hermes
locked her eyes on the golden
apple. But she knew she'd never reach it. No matter how
much she pumped her wings and clawed at the air, she
was still a flightless bird. The best she could hope for was
a long glide and a soft landing. As she plummeted, the
breeze kicked up and filled her overworked wings,
giving her a slight boost. She pumped her wings harder,
giving all she had—and just managed to make it to the
tree's lowest branch. She came to a stop in the pitch-black
leafy depths, sending twigs falling down to the ground
far below.

Athena had watched Hermes's flight. Though the
sight of the hen brought out her most basic beast

instincts, she hadn't lost her brains. Hermes might be able to glide, but cats could climb. She bolted for the tree's trunk before Hermes had even come to a stop in the lower branches.

CHAPTER 18

THE OLYMPIANS WERE STUNNED. THEY could no longer see Hermes within the enchanted apple tree, but they knew roughly where she was. Ares recovered first. "Climb!" he shouted, spitting out Poseidon's lifeline. The sea lord's helmet hit the hard ground with a thud.

"Careful, you oaf!" Poseidon protested. Not wanting to risk being tossed around like the pufferfish, Zeus and Demeter scrambled down off Ares's back.

But Ares was preoccupied with cheering on his new hen friend. "You can still get the apple, Hermes! Climb for it!"

"Will you quit rooting for that chicken?!" Zeus yelled.

The golden apple shone like a jewel atop a shriveling

crown as the shadows reached up to claim it. The Hesperides scrambled up to the top branch and surrounded the apple on three sides. Zeus held his breath. Inside the tree, Hermes pumped her wings and leapt desperately from branch to branch. She continued clawing her way higher and higher. When she finally neared the top, she spotted a pinpoint of sunlight above her.

She was so focused on the apple that she didn't hear Athena climbing up the trunk below her.

Zeus slowly let out the breath he'd been holding. Hermes wouldn't reach the apple in time. She was about to lose her shot at immortality.

But then two speckled white wings exploded through the leaves just beneath the Hesperides, sending the three fiery figures scrambling to the edges of their thin branches. Hermes had reached the top! She basked momentarily in the golden rays of sunlight and eyed the apple just above her, nearly within plucking distance. It gleamed brilliantly. Dazzled, Hermes turned her attention to the three Hesperides, who were now closing in around her and blazing brighter than ever.

"Now is the hour for your ignition," uttered

the first of the Hesperides.

"A painful end to your foolish mission," growled the second.

While they waited on the third, Hermes yelled, "Take this—it's limited edition!" and pulled the small wooden Zeus figure from beneath her wing. She threw it at the lead Hesperis.

The flaming creature squealed when it struck her in the chest.

Hermes had hoped the action figure would burst into flames, giving her just enough of a distraction to grab the apple. Instead, it slipped from the Hesperis's chest and landed on a leaf at her feet. It bore no scorch marks. She examined each of the Hesperides. "Guess y'all aren't such hot stuff," she said. Their fur seemed metallic, as if woven from gold, when it caught the waning rays of light. But as the sun set, their brilliance was extinguished by the shadows. The fiery effect had only been an illusion.

"Got no clever rhymes for me now, huh?" Hermes asked as they glared at her. She glanced again at the golden apple right above her. She reached up and plucked it from its branch, thrusting it high into the last blazing rays of the day. "Got it!" she exclaimed.

"She did it!" cheered Ares from far below, oblivious that no one else was pleased.

An elated Hermes made the mistake of glancing down to see who was cheering her on. "Urk." Her stomach lurched. She hadn't realized how far she'd climbed on her quest for the apple. The ground seemed miles away. The Olympians looked no larger than Zeus's action figure. Hermes closed her eyes, reeling and clutching the thin branches high at the top of the tree. She had no idea how she'd ever get down.

Suddenly, the branches really did lurch. Hermes opened her eyes to see Athena leaping from below. She'd already sent the Hesperides tumbling, and now she was closing in on Hermes.

The hen stood frozen atop the tree. She saw no escape other than jumping into the thin air. Hermes was caught between the wrath of the cat and her fear of heights. And unlike the Hesperides's flaming fur, Athena's claws were no harmless illusion.

Hermes took a deep breath, tucked the golden apple under her beak, and leapt into the purple sky, once again

pumping her wings with all she had. She risked a peek back and saw Athena perched awkwardly in the dark tree's uppermost branches. The next moment, the cat slipped into the enchanted tree's interior.

Hermes closed her eyes and concentrated on making a safe landing far, far away.

Back on the ground, Zeus ducked when his action figure narrowly missed his noggin. It shattered as it hit the ground, but he barely noticed. He had much bigger concerns. Hermes had completed the first labor of Hairy-clees.

CHAPTER 19

ZEUS GLUMLY PLOPPED DOWN ON THE ground. His lion cloak gave a sad little squeak. Demeter hopped over to him.

"It's too bad Hermes has such a crazy effect on Athena," the grasshopper said. "She'd make a good Olympian."

"Why? Because she crashed into a tree and grabbed an apple? Pffft," Zeus scoffed. "Beginner's luck." He hoped he sounded more convinced than he felt. Truth was, Zeus admired the hen's determination—something she had in common with Hairy-clees from the Oracle's lesson.

"Where'd Hermes head off to, do you suppose?" wondered Poseidon.

"She's probably halfway to the next challenge," Ares said, scratching idly with a hind foot. "I bet she's headed to get the belt from my buddy Hippolyta."

The other Olympians gawked at him. "How in the world would Hermes know where to find the Amazon queen?" Zeus asked. "Even I don't know that!"

"I told her," Ares said proudly. When he saw the fury etched on Zeus's face, his tail drooped. "Was I not supposed to?"

Zeus threw up his paws in frustration. "At this rate, Hermes'll be a full-fledged immortal by breakfast."

The Olympians sat in silence. Sunset was over; the only light came from the pale glow of the moon.

Demeter spoke first. "What do we tell Athena?"

"You don't have to tell me anything." Athena's voice made everyone jump as she stalked out of the shadows. "I'm way ahead of you on this."

Poseidon rolled up to the cat and asked her, "You know our king offered Hermes a spot with the Olympians if she completes the challenges?"

"Athena!" Zeus interrupted, eager to change the subject. "Why didn't you just stay on the other side of the portal like I asked?"

"I have every right to enter the northern lands, too,"

she replied, a hint of anger in her voice.

"How come you can't just leave Hermes alone?" Demeter asked.

Athena began preening the tufts of gray fur at the tips of her ears. "I may be the goddess of wisdom, but I'm still a cat and she's still a bird."

"But you're supposed to be the *smart* one," Ares said. "If anyone should be treating everything in Greece like a chew toy, it's me." He eyed Zeus's Nemean lion cloak and drooled.

Zeus waved to hush everyone. "We're getting sidetracked here." He turned to Athena. "You said you're ahead of us all on this Hermes problem?"

Athena stopped preening. "Maybe we can make this a win-win situation," she said. "Hermes said she just wants a place to belong, right?"

"That's right," Ares said enthusiastically. "She likes to live in a flock. But now she doesn't have one ..." He paused. "Unless you count me."

"A flock," Athena repeated. "Right. That's the key word here."

Zeus's eyes brightened as he watched Athena.

"There's the goddess of wisdom I know!" he said.
"Do go on."

"We Olympians can't be her flock for obvious reasons," Athena continued.

"Very obvious," Demeter said.

"I take it you have another flock in mind ... ?" Zeus prompted Athena.

"I do," the cat said, sitting tall. "Hermes is on her way to meet the queen of the Amazons, after all."

Zeus beamed as he realized what Athena had in mind. "Genius!" he shouted at the cat. "You're a genius!"

"Yeah, genius!" Ares agreed, then tilted his head. "Wait, what's going on?"

Zeus explained Athena's plan.

CHAPTER 20

THE OLYMPIANS MARCHED EAST TOWARD the village of the Amazons. The moon was nearly overhead now, casting a silver light upon the smooth stone beneath their feet. Odd structures and relics cluttered the stark landscape. Many of these relics were foreign to Zeus, although he recognized a few round boulders, disk-shaped objects, and even a ball chucker from Greece.

Zeus, Demeter, and Poseidon eyed every shadow suspiciously. They weren't nearly as familiar with the northern lands as Athena and Ares—and Athena wasn't with them to serve as a guide. She had traveled back through the portal for fear that her feline instincts might ruin everything when the group found Hermes.

As they skirted the obstacle course, Ares made a break for the ramp at its beginning. "Ooh, ooh! Watch me! Watch me!" he barked excitedly. "I can do the whole course in thirty seconds!"

"Get back here, Ares!" Zeus commanded. "We don't have thirty seconds to waste. Do I have to remind you that it's your job to lead us to Hippolyta and this mysterious tribe of Amazons?" The pug tucked his tail and returned reluctantly to the group.

"What can you tell us about these birds?" Demeter asked as they continued east.

Ares pepped up. "Oh, the Amazons are a tribe of supertough feathered warriors. They can be kind of snobby until you get to know them."

Zeus gave Ares a sideways glance. "So how'd you get to be so chummy with them?"

"Hippolyta says I'm, like, the funniest war god she knows." Ares puffed out his chest as they walked. "Oh, and I bring them snacks. Sacks and sacks of snacks when Artie isn't around."

Poseidon cracked a smile. "And suddenly this relationship makes a lot more sense."

The Olympians walked in silence until they came to a sheer cliff looming up before them. The cliff contained a secure portal that bore a sign with a faded script surrounded by strange symbols:

The Olympians couldn't read the script, but they recognized two of the symbols as lightning bolts, and a third that looked vaguely like the Minotaur: a bullish head with fearsome horns.

"The Minotaur's lair is behind that portal?" Poseidon asked. He brandished his trident defensively.

"Huh," Ares replied, as if noticing the sign for the first time. "I never gave it much thought before."

"When have you ever given much thought to anything?" Demeter asked, eyeing the door nervously. "I'm just glad it's closed!"

"We have enough on our plate tonight," Zeus said. He bent down to inspect bits of debris that littered the ground at the foot of the cliff. He picked up a piece and turned it over in his paw. It was a shell from a sunflower seed. Nearby, glittering in the moonlight, was a shred of clear crinkly material bearing an image of a smiling bird above odd markings:

Wingin' It Bird Treats

"Hey! That's the stuff I sneak out to the Amazons!" Ares nodded toward the shredded material.

"Really satisfies my need for seed," announced a voice from the shadows.

Startled, the Olympians watched Hermes emerge from

the darkness and start scratching at sunflower shells on the ground. Tucked under one wing was the apple. It glimmered slightly even in the dim light.

"Hermes!" Ares exclaimed as he ran in clumsy circles around the hen.

"Howdy, pal," Hermes said, then glanced around nervously. "That cat ain't still with ya, is she?"

"No, no, no," Zeus said reassuringly. "She insisted on giving you some personal space. But she wishes you the best."

Hermes was skeptical. "That a fact?"

"Oh, yeah," Zeus said. "In fact, us coming to find you was all her idea."

Hermes was about to ask Zeus what he meant, when Ares jostled her. "I can't believe you got the golden apple of the sunset!" he exclaimed. "We saw the whole thing!"

"Glad someone did," Hermes said, shuddering as she recalled her endless drop from the top of the tree. "I had my eyes closed pretty much the whole time."

"We also witnessed your valiant deeds, hen," announced an oddly musical voice, which seemed to come from all directions.

"Who said that?" Zeus looked at the Olympians. "You say that?" he asked Demeter.

"I said that." The singsong voice rang down from overhead.

High above them, higher even than Mount Olympus, they saw a line that stretched from the top of the cliff off to the north. A dozen birds perched atop the line in a row.

"The Amazons, I presume," Poseidon said, then whistled a stream of bubbles. "You certainly have friends in high places, Ares."

"I know, right?" Ares nodded.

The moon cast just enough light to reveal that each bird was a different species. Zeus picked out a blue jay and a cardinal. The rest of the birds were harder to identify, although he could tell from their muted colors that all 12 were female. Near the center of the flock he spotted a feathered form much larger than the others. She appeared to be a hawk or some other type of raptor. "Hippolyta," he whispered.

Suddenly, in a blur of gray feathers, a much smaller bird detached herself from the line and streaked northwest, all the way to the enchanted apple tree, before banking back in their direction. As the bird soared closer, Zeus and Hermes could see the gray was streaked with gold beneath her wings and a chest of snow-white feathers. Against these white feathers hung a silver belt.

She landed before them with a graceful flourish of her wings. A silver plume of feathers flared on her head, forming a crown that matched her belt. She nodded to Ares, ignoring Zeus, and then fixed Hermes with her charcoal eyes.

"It's an honor to meet you, brave chicken," she sang. "I'm Hippolyta, queen of the Amazons."

CHAPTER 21

ZEUS STEPPED BETWEEN HERMES AND Hippolyta before anyone could say anything. "It's an honor to meet *her*?" he fumed, jerking his thumb at Hermes. "What about me? Don't you know who I am?"

"You're Zeus, king of the gods," Hippolyta said in her strange singsong voice, a mix of words and chirps.

"You got that right." Zeus straightened up. He and Hippolyta were roughly the same height. "And you're … Well, you're not what I expected." Zeus glanced up at the hawk he'd assumed was Hippolyta still perched on the line, then back at Hippolyta. "What kind of bird are you?"

"A tufted titmouse, not that it's your business." The bird unfolded a wing and nudged Zeus, causing his cloak

to emit a humiliating squeak. "Please step aside. I wish to speak only with ..." She stared at Hermes expectantly.

"H-H-Hermes! The n-name's Hermes," Hermes stammered, still in shock that the queen of the Amazons was addressing her directly. She held a wingtip out to Hippolyta. "Uh, pleased to meet ya."

"Likewise." Hippolyta awkwardly pressed the tip of her wing against Hermes's. She cocked her head and regarded the golden apple tucked beneath Hermes's other wing. "We watched you pluck the golden apple of the sunset from under the noses of those wretched Hesperides. That was a feat worthy of Heracles!"

"Um, it's pronounced 'Hairy-clees,'" Zeus chimed in.

Hippolyta eyed Zeus. "Heracles," she repeated, pronouncing it carefully as "Hair-ah-clees."

"Shucks," Hermes said. "What I did was no big thing."

Zeus saw his chance to steer the conversation according to Athena's plan. "It wasn't just a feat worthy of *Hairy-clees*," he said, emphasizing his pronunciation. "It was worthy of the Amazons—which is precisely why I brought you two together."

Hermes guffawed. "In what world did you bring us together?"

Ignoring the question, Zeus asked Hermes, "You're searching for a flock to call your own, right?" He turned to the Amazon queen. "And you ladies are a warrior tribe. I bet you're always seeking brave fellow birds to do ... whatever brave stuff you Amazons do." He held his paws out to Hermes. "Well, Hermes here is as brave as Hairy-clees himself."

Zeus's compliment took Hermes aback. Her rubbery beard blushed. "Gosh, thanks," she said.

"Isn't this all you want?" Zeus gestured around the northern lands. "A place to belong here? And without having to do a bunch of legendary labors or worry about getting shredded by a cat?"

Hermes considered this for a moment and then nodded, her crown of stubby feathers bobbing. "That would be nice."

"Well, welcome home!"

Hippolyta jabbed a wing at Zeus. "It's not up to you to decide who can join our tribe, king of the gods," she sang. Both Zeus's and Hermes's expressions fell. "And yet ...

it just so happens I was about to offer membership to Hermes myself. We welcome all courageous birds who take wing."

Zeus's spirits soared. Athena's plan was coming together! The Amazons were about to take Hermes into their tribe—and off his hands.

CHAPTER 22

HERMES'S GRIN FADED AS SOMETHING Hippolyta had said struck home. "You said all birds who take wing? You mean fly?"

"Yes, of course," sang Hippolyta. She stretched out both wings. "Flight is a prerequisite for us. It comes with the territory." She gestured at the line high above, where all the other Amazons were perched.

"Well, then I probably oughta tell you that we hens don't exactly soar through the air with the greatest of ease," Hermes admitted. She couldn't bring herself to look at the line, which seemed miles away. Her legs felt like jelly. She hadn't fully recovered from her fall from the apple tree. "In fact, I pretty much prefer hoofin' it everywhere."

"That is … unfortunate," Hippolyta replied.

Hermes focused on her feet to steady herself. "And to be honest," she added, "I'm not a big fan of heights—"

"Okay, there," Zeus laughed, clapping a paw on Hermes's speckled shoulder. "No need to give your whole life story, pal. Plenty of time for that when you're meeting and greeting all your new Amazon buddies." He turned to Hippolyta. "I'll just leave you two to discuss the particulars about cohabitation. Now if you'll excuse me ..."

"Certainly it must be obvious that your hen friend cannot join us." Hippolyta's singsong voice took on a sad lilt. "Because she has a bit of an altitude problem."

Zeus shut his eyes and grit his teeth. "Blast it!"

Hermes's head was spinning, so she stared at the Amazon queen's silver belt, which was a nice steady point to help settle her vertigo. That's when she remembered why she had come here in the first place. "The belt," she blurted.

"Beg your pardon?" Hippolyta replied.

Hermes composed herself. "I clearly don't have the right stuff to join y'all," she said to Hippolyta, "but maybe you can help me in another way?"

"I will if I can," Hippolyta said. She followed Hermes's gaze to the silver chain wrapped around her torso.

Zeus had a bad feeling about where this was all going.

"Your belt is one of the labors that Oracle lady mentioned," Hermes explained. "Having it would get me one step closer to finding my place here. I don't suppose you'd be willing to trade?" She held out the golden apple of the sunset, which had already begun to lose its enchanted luster.

Hippolyta eyed it distastefully. "Keep your prize." She paused. "I sympathize with your situation, yet my belt is no trinket. It isn't something to be handed out like some limited-edition keepsake." She cocked her head at Zeus.

"She's talking about your action figures," Demeter whispered loudly from the sidelines.

"Not helpful," Zeus answered.

"I acquired my belt through an act of immense fearlessness," Hippolyta continued. "You would need to do the same."

"Oh, Hermes is fearless, all right," Ares chimed in. "She nearly beat the Hydra all by herself!"

"Is that so?" Hippolyta considered Hermes with one eye, then the other, turning her head with jerky movements. "Finish off the five-headed swamp monster for good, and my belt shall be yours."

Zeus panicked. "What?! You can't just give the chicken your belt!"

Hippolyta didn't bother to acknowledge his outburst.

Zeus threw his paws in the air and stormed off to the west. "Great plan, Athena," he muttered to himself. "'Maybe we can make this a win-win situation,' she said. Hermes 'just wants a place to belong,' she said. Well, now Hermes is on the fast track to immortality!"

Demeter, Poseidon, and Ares watched his tirade, unsure if they should follow him. Zeus stopped and whirled back in their direction. "What are you waiting for, Olympians? We are leaving!" He continued stomping toward the portal that led home from the northern lands.

The three Olympians exchanged awkward glances with Hermes.

"Uh, we have to go home now, buddy," Ares said. "See ya later, I hope."

"I hope so, too," Hermes answered. "Whatever happens, it was nice to meet ... most of you." She watched the Olympians race off to catch up to Zeus, then turned to Hippolyta. "I appreciate you offering me your belt and all," she said sheepishly, "but I have more than just the Hydra to deal with."

"You speak of the cat, I presume," Hippolyta said.

Hermes nodded. "Right. The cat who wants to eat me."

Hippolyta cocked her head. "Cats have been chasing birds since the age of Cronos and the Titans."

"Uh, okay," Hermes replied. "Any advice?"

Hippolyta didn't hesitate. "She can't chase you if you don't run."

CHAPTER 23

"EVERYTHING GO ACCORDING TO PLAN?"
Athena asked as her fellow Olympians clambered back through the dog-size portal, which Ares held open.

"Not exactly," Demeter said.

"Oh? Not exactly which part?" Athena was sitting at the helm of the *Argo,* which she had parked near the portal.

"The part about Hermes joining the Amazons, for one," Poseidon said as Ares lowered him to the ground by his lifeline.

Athena's mouth fell open. "That wasn't just a part. That was the whole plan."

"Oh, it gets worse," Zeus said, pushing the lion's mane

back from his head. "Hippolyta offered Hermes her belt if she defeats the Hydra."

"Beating the Hydra, nabbing Hippolyta's belt—those are the two remaining labors of Heracles," Demeter said. "If Hermes checks those off ..."

"She'll be immortal. She'll be an Olympian," Athena finished quietly.

"Not if we beat the Hydra first," Zeus announced.

"What's the plan, boss?" Ares asked eagerly.

Zeus noticed sunlight creeping across Greece. "I'll fill you in tonight. We should really all skedaddle home before Artie and Callie get here."

The Olympians scattered. Zeus and Demeter climbed the rope to the secret door of their palace. Exhausted from their long night, Zeus didn't even bother to hang up his lion cloak—he just tossed it on the floor, tumbled onto the Golden Fleece that served as his bed, and fell into a deep slumber.

CHAPTER 24

ZEUS AWOKE TO DEMETER STANDING OVER him, prodding him with four of her six legs. He was about to protest when he heard the Oracle talking.

"Once Heracles finally got the chain from Hippolyta," the Oracle was saying, "he could move on to the next labor."

"The next labor?!" Zeus hopped out of bed and ran to the pillars of his palace. The spiky fur on his head stood in all directions; despite his bedhead, he was wide awake. "There are more than three labors?"

"That's why I woke you!" Demeter joined Zeus at the edge of the palace. "I knew you'd want to hear this."

Zeus took a quick survey of Greece and saw Artie collecting more of the mossy green boulders Ares had spilled the day before. Her rectangular relic poked from her back pocket.

"In fact," the Oracle continued, "Heracles's challenges had only just begun. No fewer than nine remained."

"Nine more labors?" Zeus marveled. "Hermes isn't even close to being done!"

"Heracles next had to hunt the Nemean lion and claim its hide," the Oracle said.

"The Nemean lion?" Zeus spun and spied the lion's hide where he'd left it, on the floor by the secret back door. He cackled. "Hermes'll never complete that labor as long as I have the cloak."

"In fact, for the next series of labors," the Oracle continued, "Heracles was charged with tracking down a zoo's worth of fantastical animals. He had to capture the Cerynean hind, a sort of giant deer-like creature, and yet it was faster and more cunning than any deer. It took Heracles a year to track the animal down."

"A year?!" Demeter repeated. "Who has that kind of patience?"

"Not Hermes, I'll bet," Zeus said gleefully.

"Next, he had to hunt and capture a wild boar, which

Heracles only managed by chasing the animal into snow up to its neck."

Zeus smirked. "That might be tricky, considering it never ever snows here."

"He was also ordered to hunt down massive horses with a taste for human flesh," the Oracle explained.

Zeus's belly growled, and he reached into his bowl and began popping pieces of Fuzzy Feast into his mouth like they were popcorn.

Demeter watched Zeus eat with a sour expression. "Hardly an appetizing story, Zeus."

"What?" he said through stuffed cheeks. "I haven't eaten all day!"

The Oracle continued: "Heracles then was dispatched to Crete to vanquish a vicious bull monster."

"Bull monster? Crete?" Demeter repeated. "That rings a bell."

"Shhhh! The Oracle's talking!" Zeus hissed.

"With the bull beaten," the Oracle explained, "Heracles rustled an entire herd of cattle. And he was ordered to chase away a flock of monster birds."

"So. Many. Labors!" Zeus couldn't resist. He hopped

in his exercise wheel and started sprinting.

"Yet these challenges weren't all fun and high adventure," the Oracle said. "Each was designed to teach Heracles a lesson or fix some flaw with his personality. One of his final challenges taught humility. Heracles was given nothing more than a shovel and tasked with scooping the poop from vast stables that hadn't been cleaned in more than a hundred years."

"Ho-ho!" Zeus leapt off his wheel. "Have fun with that one, Hermes!"

"Shoveling a century's worth of cattle patties wasn't really Heracles's style," the Oracle continued. "Instead, the muscle-bound mortal used boulders to divert a river into the stables, washing away all that filth in a day."

"Oh, that was a smart move," Zeus agreed, popping another piece of Fuzzy Feast into his mouth. "This Hairy-clees definitely has some Zeus blood in him."

"Each labor was more difficult than the last, testing Heracles's determination, until finally he had to complete the most challenging task of all: to fetch the three-headed dog Cerberus from his master, Hades."

"Hades?" Demeter repeated. "I don't know a Hades, do you?"

"Who cares?" Zeus said, spitting crumbs. "What matters is it'll take forever for Hermes to get through this to-do list."

Hermes would never become immortal. She'd never become an Olympian. The team members could get back to building their mojo.

"That's all the time we have this week," the Oracle said as harp music began playing in the background. "Will Heracles finally complete his great Herculean effort? Tune in and find out." Artie's relic went quiet.

"Whoa!" Callie's startled voice broke the silence. She had just entered Greece from uncharted territory carrying a hunched, scaly form.

"Everything okay?" Artie called out from the Bugcropolis.

"Yeah, yeah," Callie said. "I nearly tripped over this dumb thing." She kicked away one of the mossy green boulders.

But Zeus didn't pay any attention to the boulder. He was locked on what Callie was carrying: the Hydra.

"What's your plan for the fan?" Artie asked as she retrieved the rolling boulder.

"I'm going to install it someplace out of the way," Callie said, "where your little Greek gods can't get to it."

"Heh, good luck with that," Zeus taunted Callie. The Oracle's lesson had left him feeling elated, recharged.

"Where's she taking that thing?" Demeter asked as she watched Callie carry the Hydra beyond the mountainside home of Kiko the dragon in northern Greece.

"Some dark corner of the realm, I'm sure." Zeus had already put on his lion cloak. Now he dug around for Hekate's torch, a relic that created magical light. "Aha!" He held it up and jabbed a rubbery bump on the torch's side, causing it to emit a blinding light from the crystal on its tip. He quickly switched it off. "Who's ready to hunt some Hydra?"

CHAPTER 25

SWEAR, ZEUS," POSEIDON SAID AS THE Olympians huddled around him in the dim light, "you're more worked up about the Hydra's return than I am. It's my realm that is most at risk."

Zeus had summoned the Olympians the moment Artie and Callie walked out the main portal for the night. Lighting the path with Hekate's torch, he had led everyone east across Greece at a trot, to where he had last seen Callie carry the Hydra.

"It's more than just your realm," Zeus said. "Our entire team's at risk!" He flashed the torch across his companions for emphasis. "Taking on the Hydra will get us Olympians back to normal."

"Should we be worried that a five-headed swamp

monster represents normal around these parts?"
Demeter asked.

Zeus ignored her. "Nothing like a five-headed swamp
monster to bring out our mojo."

"What makes you so sure that Hermes won't try to
tackle the Hydra, too?" Ares asked. "That's one of the
labor things she has to do to become immortal, right?"

"Ares, will you try listening to the Oracle's lesson
once in your life?" Zeus snapped. "She rattled off another

nine challenges. No way Hermes can do all those."

"That Hairy-clees fella did them," Ares said, "and Hermes is at least as determined as he was. Like, maybe we should call her Feathered-clees."

"Thanks, buddy," came a familiar voice, "but I prefer Hermes." Zeus swung Hekate's torch, and the light fell upon a poof of speckled feathers.

"Hermes!!" Ares ran up to the hen. "What are you doing here?"

"Takin' on the Hydra." Hermes shrugged like it was obvious. "What're y'all folks doin' here?"

"Hah! See, Zeus!" Ares yelled as he spun in a circle. "I knew Hermes wouldn't give up!"

Athena had crouched and locked her blue eyes on the hen the moment she appeared. Only the white tip of her tail moved, whipping back and forth.

"No, no, no!" Zeus stepped in front of Athena and waved his paws in the air. "Snap out of it! We don't need this drama now!"

But Athena's crazed eyes seemed to bore right through Zeus. She simply pounced over him toward the hen.

This time, though, Hermes didn't dart away. On the

contrary, she stood defiantly, wings on her hips, chest puffed out. Just as Athena was about to crash into her would-be prey, Hermes raised a wing and batted the cat aside. Athena tumbled gracefully, and then rolled to her feet. Her eyes remained focused on Hermes, but they no longer had that crazed look.

"What was *that*?" Ares exclaimed.

Athena shook her head. "Yeah, what was that?" she echoed.

"Just a little tip I picked up from the queen of the Amazons," Hermes answered. She was still standing with her wings on her hips. "Cats can't chase you if you don't run."

Athena hunched on her front legs again, preparing to pounce. Hermes in turn raised her wing, making it clear she was ready to bat down another attack. Athena uncoiled and sat normally. "Yeah, I guess that does make sense," Athena said. She seemed like her old relaxed self.

CHAPTER 26

 "SO ... ARE WE GOOD?" ZEUS ASKED carefully, glancing between Athena and Hermes.

"I'm good," answered Hermes. Though she kept her eyes on the cat.

Athena had busied herself cleaning the bracelet on one of her paws when she noticed everyone staring at her. "Oh, I'm good," she said.

"Um ... okay, then." Zeus adjusted his laurel-wreath crown. "So maybe you didn't hear the Oracle's lesson," he said to Hermes, "but you have a lot more labors to accomplish before you can become an Olympian. Like, a *ton* more."

"It is a rather long list," Poseidon chimed in. "No one

would fault you for becoming discouraged."

"Who's discouraged?" Hermes asked. "If that Hairy-clees fella could do them, so can I."

"Yeah." Ares nodded enthusiastically. "What she said."

"If doin' these things is the only way to join all y'all," Hermes said, "then that's what I gotta do. Besides, I think y'all might need me for this labor."

"Need you?" Zeus scoffed. "For what?"

"Have y'all seen where the Hydra has gotten to?" Hermes asked. "He's in a real pickle of a spot."

The Olympians had come to a long plateau. Up above, Zeus could see the green boulders Artie and Callie had collected there, along with ancient tomes emblazoned with blue jays, parrots, cardinals, and other birds in flight—tomes celebrating the exploits of the Amazons, he presumed. But there was no sign of a five-headed swamp monster.

"Probably easier if I just show ya. That light," she said, pointing to Hekate's torch, "mind if I borrow it?"

Zeus handed it to her. Hermes fumbled with it until she figured out how to switch it off. She turned east and stalked into the darkness. The Olympians all followed, with Athena keeping a respectful distance.

The group didn't go far before Hermes stopped and propped the back of the torch on the ground and aimed its crystal tip toward the sky. "Y'all need to see what we're dealing with," she said ominously as the others gathered around. She pushed the rubber nub on the torch's side. Light gleamed from the tip, illuminating a broad section of tiles high above.

"We're dealing with the ceiling?" Demeter asked, perplexed.

"Oh, apologies." Hermes adjusted the torch artifact downward; its light shifted lower and lower.

"GAAHHH!" The Olympians screamed in unison. Poseidon dove so hard to the bottom of his helmet, it rolled into Zeus, who fell into Hermes, who lost her grip on the torch. Above them, light danced crazily across the Hydra. Its necks, shiny with slimy scales, writhed and pulsed. Beneath its necks, a crystal on the Hydra's chest dazzled in the torchlight.

Just when the Hydra seemed about to attack, the creature settled into stillness. It had fallen back asleep.

CHAPTER 27

HERMES HAD SWITCHED OFF HEKATE'S torch, but everyone could see the Hydra plainly in the moonlight filtering across Greece. Zeus studied the slumbering monster along with the other Olympians. Then he stared off into the distance, the white patch on his cheek twitching. Zeus's mind was racing, but it was taking him nowhere.

"I thought the Hydra was a swamp monster?" Ares asked. "How'd it get way up there?"

"You'll have to ask your buddy Callie," Zeus said. "She's the one who put it there. Said she wanted to keep it safe from us. Can you imagine?"

"What's the plan, Zeus?" Poseidon asked.

There was an awkward silence while the Olympians

waited for him to respond. When he didn't, Demeter offered, "According to the Oracle's lesson, Heracles walloped the Hydra's heads until they quit growing back."

"I'm all for walloping Hydra heads," Zeus agreed, "except said heads are up there"—he waved at the sleeping Hydra—"and I'm down here. If only I still had my aegis, I could zip up there in a jiff!" Zeus waved his right forearm where he once wielded an enchanted shield that doubled as a grappling hook.

"You certain you could handle that beast on your own?" Athena asked.

"Of course!" Zeus boasted. "Don't forget I'm tricked out like Hairy-clees himself." He ran his paws down his lion cloak. "With this thing on, I'm indestructible."

Demeter eyed Zeus's ragged cloak skeptically and glanced around for anything else that might come in handy. Her eyes landed on a rack of ropes hanging nearby. Suspended above the rack was an image of a dog and some unreadable script:

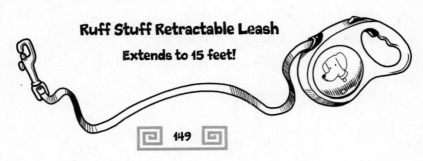

Ruff Stuff Retractable Leash

Extends to 15 feet!

Athena considered her fellow Olympians. "Zeus, I'm afraid none of us immortals can get you where you need to go."

"Told y'all you'd need me for this," Hermes said.

Zeus looked helplessly at Athena, but the cat only nodded toward Hermes and shrugged. "The chicken is right."

Zeus threw up his paws. "Hermes is bad at flying. At best she's good at falling. And besides, she's a big chicken when it comes to heights."

"She is a big chicken," Ares observed.

"But she *can* fly when she really needs to," Demeter corrected Zeus. "Kind of. We all saw it when she got the golden apple of the sunset."

"It ain't *not* true—all I need is a boost," Hermes said. "I might have a few other tricks up my wing, too."

"Oh, what does it matter?" Zeus sat down in a huff. "It's not like this operation will ever get off the ground."

"Off the ground ... " Athena repeated, squinting up at the plateau. "Hermes, you say you need a boost. That a high enough boost for you?"

Hermes studied the plateau, but it seemed far out of

reach. "Maybe, if I could get up there."

"Ares," Athena called to the pug. "Your hen friend needs a lift. Help her up there."

"You bet!" Ares dashed to Hermes and bent low. "Hop on!" he barked.

Hermes saw the plan coming together. "Not without my passenger!" She exploded into action, scooping Zeus up with her beak and plopping the hamster on her feathery back.

"Whoa, hey!" Zeus hollered, clutching the hen's feathers to keep from tumbling.

Just as he settled in, Demeter appeared at their sides dragging a long rope with a clip at its end. She held it up to Zeus. "What's this?" he asked, reaching down for the clip.

"Consider it your lifeline," she said. The rope snaked a few inches along the ground into a black box upon which Poseidon had rolled his dive helmet. "Think you can anchor it, Poseidon?" Demeter asked.

"I know a thing or two about lifelines," the pufferfish said confidently.

The plan was set. Everyone was in position.

Zeus nodded a go-ahead, and Hermes hopped atop Ares's Spartan war helmet. "Going up!" the pug barked. With one powerful kick of his muscular hind legs, Ares leapt, bringing Hermes and her passenger high enough to move onto the plateau. It was wide open except for the tall tomes featuring Amazon images and the mossy boulders gathered at the far end.

Hermes ran to that end of the plateau and stretched her wings. "Ready for takeoff?"

"No," Zeus said, "but at least with this I can't get hurt." He pulled his lion cloak tightly around him.

"Yee-haw," Hermes whooped. "Takeoff!" The hen bounded along the plateau. The mop of stubby feathers atop her head blew into Zeus's face and tickled his nose. He hunched forward, planting his head against her neck. Hermes pumped her wings, creating a blast of wind that scattered the Amazon tomes, sending a few tumbling off the plateau. "Passengers, please fasten your seat belts!"

"What's a seat belt?!" Zeus shouted as they dropped off the plateau's edge.

CHAPTER 28

HERMES SOARED THROUGH THE AIR, HER wings clawing at nothing. "I'm flying! I'm flying!" she shouted.

"You're flying! You're flying!" the Olympians cheered. Everyone except for Zeus, who still had his face buried in Hermes's feathers. His lion cloak billowed behind him like a cape.

The hen's mad flapping had a panicked quality—like she was drowning in midair. But it was enough to carry them toward the sleeping Hydra. Zeus still clutched the rope. It trailed behind them to earth far below, unspooling from the black box beneath Poseidon.

When she'd reached her maximum altitude, Hermes chanced a glance down to see if they had enough slack in the rope. "Uh-oh," she muttered, squeezing her eyes shut. Greece spun before her, and her wings began to sputter. "Why'd I do that?"

"What'd you say?" Zeus's voice was muffled by the feathers. "We're going down?" He sat bolt upright—just in time to smack into the crystal on the Hydra's chest. *SQUEAK!* Zeus clung to the crystal while Hermes continued on. Zeus's Nemean cloak absorbed the brunt of the shock but had let out its loudest squeak yet— loud enough to awaken the Hydra. Above Zeus, five pairs of eyelids on five scaly necks opened inside the cage-like helmet.

The king of the gods struggled to get a firmer grip around the crystal. He dangled from it with one arm, his other arm holding Poseidon's rope.

"You ... you got this, Zeus!" Hermes shouted as she banked hard to the side and glided back toward earth, her eyes shut tight. "It's all you!"

All five scaly necks were whirling around the beast's stocky torso, slowly at first and then faster, faster, just like before. Wind tugged at Zeus's fur as he pulled himself atop the crystal. He stood on it awkwardly, gripping the wire of the Hydra's helmet above him with one hand. He was just inches below the monster's whirling heads. Mouths on each yawned open, revealing fangs dripping with that same smelly slobber that had puddled on the beach at their first encounter.

"Yech." Zeus shuddered as he dodged droplets of drool. The Hydra's heads whirled even faster, creating a gale that turned the slobber into a mist, soaking Zeus's cloak and making everything slick. Weighed down by the wet lion's hide, Zeus began to lose his one-handed grip. He still held the end of Poseidon's rope with his other hand, but he wasn't sure what to do with it.

Zeus started to panic. Looking to the other Olympians for help, he found Hermes, who had rejoined the team after her long glide down. She gave Zeus a subtle nod, then turned toward the portal to the northern lands and threw back her head. "*Brach-crock-a-doodle-doooo!*"

Hermes's song rang out across the plains of Greece, echoing off every mountainside, down every valley. When it faded, a new sound took its place: the flapping of wings.

CHAPTER 29

ZEUS REGISTERED SHAPES STREAKING in from the west—blurs of reds, whites, browns, and greens. He decided he was delirious from struggling to hold on to the Hydra against its furious foggy gale. But as the blurs soared closer, Zeus made out the different species: a blue jay, a cardinal, a brown thrasher, a mockingbird, a massive raptor. A much smaller bird led the formation, gray with streaks of gold beneath her wings and a chest of snow-white feathers. Hippolyta was guiding her Amazons in a charge against the Hydra, and Hermes had summoned her.

The Olympians on the ground watched the Amazons storming from the west in wonder. "I guess Ares isn't the only one with friends in high places," Poseidon said.

"Hermes did say she had a few tricks up her wing," Athena added.

The Amazon squadron blew past the tall tomes that bore their images on the covers. They dove low over the scattered green boulders at the plateau's edge. Each Amazon grasped a boulder with her feet, then rose into the night sky. They banked toward the Hydra in a formation, Hippolyta in the lead.

Zeus felt a flush of elation as he realized the Amazons were targeting the Hydra for a bombing raid—but the elation was short-lived. Zeus also realized he was directly in the target zone.

The monster's five heads raged above him. They swiveled to aim their foul fog at the Amazon flock, which was closing in fast. Zeus made eye contact with Hippolyta, and he could've sworn she winked at him. "Bombs away!" she sang in her familiar singsong voice.

One after another, the birds released their payloads. The boulders sailed through the air toward the Hydra's chest. Zeus used his last bit of strength to lift his feet off the crystal, hoisting himself closer to the Hydra's helmet and out of the boulders' path.

BOP! BOP! BOP! BOP! BOP! A dozen boulder missiles pummeled the crystal.

"Bull's-eye!" Hippolyta sang as she and her squadron peeled upward past Zeus—close enough to buffet him with their wings. Above him, the Hydra's five spinning heads slowed. The gale winds decreased. Zeus firmed up his grip on the Hydra's helmet.

The Amazons banked west, buzzing low over the Olympians. Hippolyta whistled at Hermes. With a midair flourish, the Amazon queen removed her silver belt and dropped it at Hermes's feet. "I trust you can take the Hydra from here," Hippolyta sang down to Hermes. "You have earned my treasure." The hen picked up the belt and stared at it.

The Amazons continued west and glided out through the dog-size portal to the northern lands. The massive raptor—the one Zeus once mistook for Hippolyta —held the portal open for her flock until every last Amazon had returned home.

CHAPTER 30

THE AMAZONS' AIR RAID HAD BOUGHT ZEUS a chance. The Hydra was weakened. Its five heads spun sluggishly above him, barely raising a breeze strong enough to ripple Zeus's lion cloak.

"The cloak?" Zeus thought. "Right! The cloak!"

Clinging to the Hydra's helmet with one paw, Zeus yanked off his cloak and tossed it at the monster's heads. The move caused the rope to slip from his grip, but Zeus managed to stick out his toe and snag the clip at the rope's end. His toe was still sore from kicking the boulder earlier, but Zeus focused his attention on the cloak above him. It had landed on the Hydra's wire helmet and was beginning to slide off. Zeus held his breath. In the next instant, the cloak slipped through the helmet's bars and

dropped directly onto the Hydra's spinning heads—
exactly what Zeus had hoped for.

SQUEAK! The cloak immediately got tangled in the
Hydra's whirling necks. They froze with a horrible shriek
that made the Olympians cover their ears. All except for
Zeus. He didn't dare loosen his one-handed grip on the
helmet. The Hydra's entire body was shaking now.

Zeus had to escape. With his last ounce of strength,
he pulled his foot up to his chest and grabbed the rope's
clip with one paw. He worked the clip onto a wire in the
Hydra's helmet and bellowed up at the monster,
"Next time pick the easy way!" Then Zeus fell away,
sliding down the rope with both paws.

The Olympians clustered below, ready to break
his fall. They shouldn't have worried. He landed softly
and rolled.

"What are you waiting for, gang?!" Zeus shouted.
"Grab that rope and pull!"

Ares and Athena followed his order, yanking the rope
with all their might.

Above the Hydra's shrieks, the Olympians heard
something else: a low creaking sound. The beast's five

necks were still tangled by the lion cloak. Zeus swore he saw smoke rising from the center of the monster's body.

"Don't stop!" Poseidon yelled, watching the Hydra above as the Olympians pulled. "Haul away, Olympians! Haul away!"

Demeter hopped behind Athena and tugged at her leg. Zeus ran behind Ares and pulled on his tail. All the Olympians combined their strength to pull on the rope attached to the Hydra's helmet.

The creaking got louder and louder.

"Here it comes!" Hermes shouted excitedly.

POP! The Hydra detached from the wall and crashed to earth.

CHAPTER 31

THE STREET IN FRONT OF MOUNT OLYMPUS Pet Center was usually deserted when Artie arrived every morning at 8 a.m., but today she watched a beat-up pickup pull up in front of the shop. The driver's-side door bore the words "Callista's Construction Company" above an illustration of a monkey wielding a wrench. Out stepped Callie carrying her bag stuffed with tools.

"You're here bright and early," Artie said as Callie kicked the door of her truck shut.

"It's drywall day in the expansion," Callie answered as she followed Artie to the front door. "That's sweaty work. Figured I'd come in early before it got too hot. Besides, I'm dying to see what trouble your critters got into overnight."

"Oh, sheesh, I know, right?" Artie grimaced. "What'll it be this morning? Maybe Zeus building a stadium out of the cat beds?"

"I'm gonna guess Ares knocking over the bug house."

"Now you're giving me anxiety."

"Take a deep breath," Callie said. "Whatever they did, I can fix it." She hefted her tool bag and winked.

Artie laughed nervously. "You ready?" She put her key in the front door's lock. "One, two, three!"

Artie opened the door and leapt inside. "Caught ya, Olympians!" she yelled into the dim center.

All was quiet. Callie stepped in behind her and set down her bag. Both women scanned the kennels and habitats, doing a visual roll call of the animals.

"Ares is snug at home doing his thing," Callie said, pointing to his kennel beside the door. Inside, Ares was nibbling at an itch on his backside. He gazed up at her and panted, spitting slobber.

"Athena is zonked." Artie nodded toward the gray cat curled up in her bed in the corner. At the sound of her name, Athena purred and stretched out her legs, then settled on her back.

"Your prized pufferfish is in the right spot." Callie waved toward the aquariums in the middle of the center. Poseidon cruised beneath the surface with his usual retinue of seahorses. At the tank's bottom, shrimp schooled around a plastic diving helmet, busily cleaning it.

Artie laughed. "I'd be pretty shocked if Poseidon ever got out."

"Looks like all the bugs are in their bug house." Callie nodded toward the Bugcropolis.

"Dare I say there's no drama this morning?" Artie sounded hopeful. "Wait, where's Zeus?"

The bed of golden fleece in the hamster habitat, high on its shelf above the cash register, was vacant. "Maybe I spoke too soon," Artie said.

They headed toward Zeus's home, when an earsplitting sound pierced the silence: *"Brawk-a-doodle-do!"*

Both women turned to see Hermes standing below the aquarium tanks with her head thrown back, crowing at the ceiling. Guidebooks about birds were scattered around her on the floor, along with most of the tennis balls Artie and Callie had collected after Ares knocked over their display the other day.

"That's one funky chicken," Callie laughed. "What's that wrapped around her body?"

Callie and Artie approached Hermes, who was now clucking softly. Artie bent down and touched a silver chain that wrapped around the hen's chest like a sash.

"Where'd you get that, little lady?" Artie ran her fingers along the metal. "It suits you."

Callie put her hand on Artie's shoulder. "Artie, the fan. Where is it? Did … did someone break in and steal your fan?"

"What fan?"

"The floor fan I hung on the wall last night so your critters wouldn't mess with it. It's gone." She waved to the spot high in the corner where she had installed the fan. In its place was a jagged hole and a dangling mounting bracket. Below it, a large puddle had formed on the floor.

Artie was already searching the center. "Found it."

The fan—or what was left of it—was crammed into a nook between two counters on the other side of the fish tanks. Its plastic motor housing on the back was split open. The metal cage around the fan blades was dented and broken. The water reservoir for its misting system was cracked and empty. Clipped to the screen's bottom was a retractable dog leash from a nearby display.

Artie was about to unclip the leash when a chunk of golden fur tangled in the blades caught her eye. She reached in and tugged at it. It gave a sad little squeak when she pulled it free.

"Oh no, that's not one of your critters, is it?" Callie asked as Artie examined the furry lump.

"Relax," Artie said, smiling. "Just a chew toy." She held it out so Callie could see, then squeezed it. *SQUEAK!*

The toy was worn, but Callie could recognize a little fluffy tail and a lion's mane. "It certainly got chewed up, all right. How'd it get in the fan?"

Artie and Callie simultaneously leaned backward to peek around the fish tanks at Hermes. The hen blinked at them innocently, clucking away.

Artie gazed up to see Zeus watching from the bars of his habitat. "Oh," Artie said. "Zeus is in his home after all."

Callie shook her head and crossed the center to get her tool bag. "You ever think about rescuing normal animals?"

Artie smiled. "Where's the fun in that?"

CHAPTER 32

ZEUS COULDN'T REMEMBER THE LAST TIME he had been so excited to begin the night's adventures. The day had dragged by. Artie and her meddlesome friend had finally left for the night, and now Zeus stood in the Agora with Demeter.

"Let's get this show on the road." Zeus cupped his paws around his mouth, preparing to holler for the rest of the Olympians to assemble.

Then he paused and turned to the speckled hen, who was roosting atop one of the Agora's rope-wrapped pillars. "This should really be your job from now on," Zeus said. "Aren't you the messenger of the gods?"

In answer, Hermes hopped down from the pillar, shook out her wings, and threw back her head. Her chest puffed up against the silver belt draped across it. "*Brach-crock-a-doodle-doooo!*" Hermes's song echoed across the landscape.

Zeus, Demeter, and Hermes waited for what felt like a long time. Finally, "Hermes! Hermes! Hermes!" Ares barked as he came barreling across the plains of Greece, his helmet barely hanging on to the back of his head. He ran around the hen in circles, then stopped and bowed playfully in front of her. "Did you summon us for tonight's adventure?!"

"That's my job, apparently," the hen said.

THUMP. The Olympians turned to the Aegean Sea and saw that Poseidon had touched down in his dive helmet. He rolled quickly to the Agora and saluted Hermes with his trident. "That song of yours travels frightfully well underwater." He tapped his fin against the side of his head and opened and closed his mouth, as if clearing an ear.

"Good to know," Hermes said. "Maybe I can tone it down a little—"

Athena dropped suddenly into the middle of the Agora. She sunk low on her front paws and fixed Hermes with her blue eyes, her tail twitching. Hermes stood tall

and returned Athena's glare defiantly. Everyone waited nervously. Zeus's cheek patch began to twitch.

In a flash, Athena lashed out and sunk her claws into one of the Agora's pillars behind the hen. "Good to see Zeus is putting your talents to good use," she said as she began scratching vigorously at the post with both claws. "I was going to suggest you summon us from now on."

The rest of the Olympians relaxed, and Ares turned to Zeus. "So you're really letting Hermes join us Olympians, boss?"

"What can I say?" Zeus shrugged. "The chicken's a regular Hairy-clees."

"You mean Feathered-clees?" Ares suggested helpfully.

"Again, I'm good with Hermes," the hen said.

"We couldn't have beaten the Hydra without her," Demeter said.

"Let's not get too carried away," Zeus added. "The Amazons did help."

"We all helped," Poseidon declared. "Why, I've never seen our team operate at such peak efficiency."

"Nothing like a five-headed swamp monster to bring out our mojo," Demeter muttered, grinning.

Athena dashed off into the dim landscape, and Ares began running circles around Hermes again. "You can live in my chambers, buddy! We can eat Mutt Nuggets, and go play on my obstacle course, and tell scary stories, and eat Mutt Nuggets, and—"

"You two figure out your roommate situation later," Zeus interrupted. "We have a more pressing practical matter to settle."

"Like the fact that I'm still a mortal?" Hermes asked.

"Bingo!" Zeus snapped his fingers. "You need to finish Hairy-clees's labors before you can officially join us."

"Aww, right." Ares had settled down. "How many are left?"

"Gosh, let me think." Hermes rubbed her rubbery beard. "So far I got the golden apple and Hippolyta's belt, we beat the Hydra ... I need to track down what's left of that lion cloak, clean some stables, and some other stuff ..."

"How about instead of standing around talking about the labors, we just go do them?" Demeter suggested.

"Awesome idea!" Ares's curly tail was a blur. "You should get the Amazons to help, too," he said to Hermes.

"I don't know about that," the hen said. "Hippolyta made it clear I should only call on them for emergencies."

"We don't need those birds," Zeus said. "We've got so much mojo right now, we'll have these labors taken care of by midnight."

Athena rolled up on the *Argo*. "All aboard, Olympians. We have an immortal to make and moonlight's wasting."

THE TRUTH BEHIND THE FICTION

Land of Heroes

If you went back in time 2,500 years and asked for directions to ancient Greece, you would get a lot of confused stares. Ancient Greece wasn't a country or kingdom with precise borders—it was an entire civilization that flourished near the Aegean and Mediterranean Seas. Yet the people who lived in this time and place enjoyed something that might be familiar today: Ancient Greeks loved tales about superpowered heroes overcoming incredible odds and defeating villains. They didn't have comic books or movies, of course. Instead, traveling singers and poets journeyed from city to city and shared these entertaining myths with rapt audiences.

What Is a Myth?

A myth is a special kind of story told to help people make sense of their world in the days before science and internet search engines. Why does the sun set? Why does the earth quake? Where did the world come from? Myths offered supernatural solutions to these

Olympian gods had their own colossal temples. This one, built for Zeus in Athens, once had more than a hundred columns.

mysteries by explaining that a squad of gods and goddesses, from Ares to Zeus, pulled the universe's strings. Ancient Greeks took these stories for fact, building temples and holding lavish events to appease the gods. The original Olympic Games were actually created in honor of Zeus.

Origin Stories

The Greek myths are so old they were told out loud—as poems and songs—before they were even written down. The tales weren't put on paper until after 800 B.C., when a poet named Homer composed his two epic poems, the *Iliad* and the *Odyssey*. These tales were an account of a conflict called the Trojan War and featured Greek gods and mortal humans. Homer didn't bother giving origin stories for his characters because ancient Greeks already knew all about them from their own songs and poems.

Heroic Journeys

Even after the civilization of ancient Greece came under Roman rule more than 2,000 years ago, Greek culture lived on and its myths were not forgotten. The Romans simply adapted the tales for their own use. Modern-day authors, playwrights, and screenwriters do the same thing, tweaking and retelling myths for audiences.

Today, Greek mythology's influence can be found everywhere from movies to store names and clothing brands. The Greeks' myths established the "hero's journey"—a formula featured in stories ranging from Star Wars to Harry Potter: a hero yearning for adventure, a series of dangerous trials, help or hindrance from the supernatural, and victory over impossible odds. Sound familiar?

Athena marches in the middle of a parade of gods on this ancient Greek vase.

The ancient Greeks worshipped 12 major gods known as the Olympians (because they gathered on Mount Olympus, the highest peak in ancient Greece). These gods were all-powerful, and yet in some ways they were relatable. The Olympians possessed the same emotions—love, sadness, anger, jealousy—as everyday mortals.

Zeus

King of the gods, leader of the Olympians, Zeus ruled from Mount Olympus and held domain over the heavens and the land beneath them. He brought order, making sure the sun rose every day and none of his fellow gods got out of line.

Poseidon

God of all bodies of water—from the mightiest ocean to the piddliest puddle—Poseidon commanded the tides and calmed tropical storms using his enchanted trident. Sailors prayed to him for safe passage. He was a brother to Zeus. Like some siblings, they didn't always get along.

Athena

Goddess of wisdom, Athena was the brains of the Olympian operation, having outwitted Poseidon and even Zeus at various times. She also inspired creativity. When ancient Greeks wanted to build something—from a wagon to a ship—they prayed to Athena for inspiration.

Ares

Few Greek gods were as feared as Ares, the god of war. He was a brute, a force of chaos. He attacked first and asked questions ... never! Warriors screamed his name before charging into battle.

Demeter

As the goddess of food and harvests, Demeter was beloved by ancient Greeks. One bad season of crops could lead to disaster. Demeter kept everyone's belly full.

Artemis

A guardian and caretaker, and a crack shot with her bow, Artemis was the goddess of animals, protecting the young and helpless. She lived in the wilderness, tending to her furry and feathered friends.

Hermes

With his feathered sandals and winged hat, Hermes was the most graceful of the Olympian gods, which is one reason they chose him as their messenger. Yet he also had a mischievous side and mingled with the mortals. They prayed to him when they needed wit, trickery, or even a good night's sleep.

AMAZING ARTIFACTS

Greek mythology is rich with relics enchanted with astounding powers.

Nemean Cloak

The ancient Greek region of Nemea was the home to a monster lion whose hide was impervious to weapons. Heracles the hero was charged with subduing it and saving the locals. He wrestled it into submission and wore its hide as a trophy. The hide made Heracles equally indestructible.

Hekate's Torch

Though she wasn't an Olympian, Hekate was a goddess of witchcraft, always depicted carrying two torches, which were symbols of her power and a source of unending light.

The Myth of Heracles

From Achilles to Ariadne, Greek mythology is full of amazing mortals, but none of them tops the mighty Heracles when it comes to confidence or cultural appeal through the centuries. This brawny action hero showed bravery at an early age. Heracles was just a baby when two poisonous snakes slithered into his crib and reared up to strike his half brother, Iphicles. Heracles struck first, bashing the snakes senseless. Heracles's parents found him playing with the snakes like they were toys, giggling and fearless. They realized there was something special about their son. In truth, he wasn't really their son at all.

Kid Zeus

Heracles's real dad was Zeus, king of the gods. Yet Heracles inherited none of the limitless powers and immortality of his father. Instead, he was born with big muscles and a thick head. His human parents hired the finest tutors to teach young Heracles history, art, and music. The boy didn't know his own strength. He crushed musical instruments to splinters and committed even worse misdeeds—always by mistake. Soon, Heracles developed a reputation as a brute, always hurting those around him. He wanted to find a way to undo his mistakes.

The Labors of Heracles

He sought advice from the Oracle at Delphi, who told him he might find forgiveness if he completed ten labors—special challenges that would prove impossible for most mortals. These labors tested his strength, his cleverness, and his humility. He had to hunt a lion that was terrorizing the countryside of Nemea. Arrows bounced off the beast's hide, so Heracles wrestled it into submission and then wore the beast's indestructible hide to help in later labors. He had to slay a many-headed swamp beast: the Hydra. For this quest he sought help from his cousin—a violation of the rules. And so another labor was added. He was tasked with mucking out stables that hadn't been cleaned in a century. Heracles diverted a river to wash away the filth. Yet that was considered cheating, so a twelfth labor was added!

But Heracles was nothing if not determined. He carried on. Many of his labors involved tracking exotic and dangerous animals: an enchanted deer, a flock of toxic birds, a bold bull in Crete, man-eating horses. He traveled to the land of the Amazons, a fierce tribe of women warriors, to get the belt of their queen, Hippolyta. Finally he faced his most difficult labor: fetching the three-headed dog Cerberus, guard hound of the underworld. Of course he succeeded.

Beginning of the End

Heracles's life wasn't all labors and no play. He had many adventures. He made many friends. He cracked jokes. He partied. And in the end he got what he wanted—forgiveness—and more. When he rose to the heavens to join the Olympian gods, he was granted immortality, becoming a god himself.

SERBIA

KOSOVO

NORTH MACEDONIA

ALBANIA

Mount Olympus ◆

ITALY

ADRIATIC SEA

GREECE

TYRRHENIAN SEA

IONIAN SEA

Delphi ●

Corinth
Nemea ●
Argos ●

Sparta ●

Athens, Georgia, United States

Athens, Greece

Athens, Georgia, is about 5,600 miles (9,000 km) away from Athens, Greece.

↑ *Strait of Messina*

SICILY

The highest peak in ancient Greece, Mount Olympus was where Zeus held court over the Olympians.

At the height of its power around 800 B.C., ancient Greece was a sprawling empire. While its geography divided it into many separate regions, they all shared the same language, culture, and— most important—mythology.

Argos, one of the oldest cities in the world, was once home to the Hydra. The many-headed monster stalked the swamps around Argos, attacking the unwary with its venomous bite.

MAP KEY
◆ Ancient location
● Ancient city
▉ Area controlled by Greece around 500 B.C.
— Present-day boundary

MED

0 ——— 100 miles
0 ——— 100 kilometers

To Colchis →

BULGARIA

BLACK SEA

T U R K E Y

Sea of Marmara

Troy

AEGEAN SEA

Thebes

Athens

Miletus

Nemea was a spring-fed paradise of valleys and meadows until a fearsome lion emerged from caves high up on a hillside. The Nemean lion terrified the countryside until Heracles vanquished the beast as one of his labors.

According to the Heracles myth, the Amazon tribe of female warriors lived near the Black Sea, in modern Turkey.

Sea of Crete

C R E T E

Knossos

ITERRANEAN SEA

BOOK 4:

The Epic Escape From the Underworld

Z EUS THE MIGHTY WISHED HE HAD NEVER
sneaked away from home. For the first night in
as long as he could remember, his squad of
Olympian gods didn't have an adventure awaiting them:
no multiheaded monsters to vanquish, no enchanted
relics to recover, no perilous journeys to undertake.

Instead, the Olympians milled about in the Agora
while Zeus leaned against a rope-wrapped pillar, glancing
longingly up at his palace. He could be on Mount Olympus
now, kicking back in his Golden Fleece bed, popping pieces
of Fuzzy Feast into his mouth.

"Watch us, Zeus! Watch! Watch!" A tan pug barreled past the king of the Greek gods, snapping him out of his daydream.

"Watch what?" Zeus straightened his royal chiton as Ares the pug continued his mad scramble. The hamster's mouth dropped when he noticed a white speckled hen perched precariously on Ares's back. "Why is Hermes riding on Ares, Demeter?" Zeus asked the grasshopper lazing nearby.

"Beats me," replied Demeter, the goddess of the harvest and Zeus's best friend. She paid little mind to the charging pug as she nibbled on a piece of lettuce hung around her neck.

"I believe he's trying to help Hermes fly," explained Athena the cat, who was batting at a feather hanging from the tip of a springy stick standing upright from a rubber cup stuck to the ground. Artie had given Athena the toy recently to help distract her from chasing Hermes. Athena might be the goddess of wisdom, but she was still a cat, and cats chased birds.

Zeus observed as Ares ran in a wide arc that brought him back in their direction. He now charged full speed at the assembled Olympians, his wrinkly face hidden by his Spartan war helmet. On his back, Hermes held her wings out for balance, like a surfer riding a wave.

Poseidon the pufferfish, floating in his clear dive helmet, eyed the approaching pair with growing concern. "Should we move, perhaps?" The pug was mere feet away with no sign of slowing.

"Ares!" Zeus yelled, raising his paws and standing directly in the pug's path. "Pump the brakes!"

"Stop, stop, STOP!" Poseidon held up his trident.

But Ares wasn't stopping. Athena and Demeter leapt out of the way just as the dog was about to blast through the Olympians like a pug-shaped bowling ball. Zeus and Poseidon braced for impact.

At the last second, though, Ares dug all four paws into the ground and skidded to a halt inches from Zeus and Poseidon. Hermes kept going, catapulted off the pug's back. She pumped her wings clumsily and clawed higher and higher into the air.

It wasn't an impressive performance by most bird standards, but for a chicken, she positively soared.

"Go, go, go!" Ares encouraged, panting to catch his breath.

"Stretch your wings more!" Athena shouted, no longer interested in her toy. "You'll get more lift!"

"No, flutter your wings like this!" Poseidon yelled, wiggling his pectoral fins to demonstrate.

"I think I know more about flying than y'all!" Hermes hollered back.

The Olympians noticed that Hermes had her eyes squeezed tight against her fear of heights.

"Flying blind might not be the best idea," Ares shouted. He had pushed his Spartan war helmet back on his head so that his wrinkly pug face poked out. "Oh, watch out!"

BOOM!

Hermes had flown straight into the portal to uncharted territory. But instead of just smacking against it, she had knocked it open and continued right into the mysterious realm beyond.

"I did *not* see that coming!" Zeus said, suddenly excited.

"I don't think Hermes did, either," Demeter added.

For the first time in more than a month, the entryway to uncharted territory stood open.

Acknowledgments

Writing an adventure series is an adventure itself—complete with a cast of indispensable allies. Becky Baines at National Geographic Kids dreamed up the idea of Mount Olympus Pet Center and invited me to embark on this quest. Kate Hale led the charge and never let the adventure drag. Catherine Frank—oracle of children's literature—found the most exciting narrative paths for us to explore.

Illustrator Andy Elkerton continues to bring our Olympian heroes (and their foes) to vivid life, while design director Amanda Larsen creates the cool look for each book. Production editor Molly Reid makes sure I write right while ensuring the world of Mount Olympus Pet Center is portrayed consistently from the first page to the last. Photo director Lori Epstein lends her expert eye.

Dr. Diane Harris Cline, a professor of history and classics at George Washington University and an expert on all things Greek, is my beacon for staying within sight of the source material. She's written the book on ancient Greece. Literally. It's called *The Greeks: An Illustrated History* and was as valuable to me in this process as any of Zeus's relics.

Finally, my wife, Ramah, is an endless source of inspiration and patience. She's also the wisest person I know when it comes to chickens (we live on a farm). Our brave chicken Odo was almost certainly the inspiration for Hermes the hen.

—*Crispin Boyer*

All artwork by Andy Elkerton/Shannon Associates LLC unless otherwise noted below:
180, Pamela Loreto Perez/Shutterstock; 181 (UP), kanvag/Shutterstock; 181 (LO), Rogers Fund, 1906/Metropolitan Museum of Art; 182 (UP LE), DeAgostini/Getty Images; 182 (UP RT), Luisa Ricciarini/Leemage/Universal Images Group/Getty Images; 182 (LO LE), Harris Brisbane Dick Fund, 1950/Metropolitan Museum of Art; 182 (LO RT), Prisma Archivo/Alamy Stock Photo; 183 (UP LE), adam eastland/Alamy Stock Photo; 183 (UP CTR), The Cesnola Collection, Purchased by subscription, 1874-76/Metropolitan Museum of Art; 183 (UP RT), Fletcher Fund, 1925/Metropolitan Museum of Art; 183 (LO LE), Gift of Mrs. Frederick F. Thompson, 1903/Metropolitan Museum of Art; 183 (LO RT), The Bothmer Purchase Fund, 1987/Metropolitan Museum of Art; 184, Ashmolean Museum, University of Oxford, UK/Bridgeman Images; 184-185, Andrey Kuzmin/Shutterstock